The Were[...]
of Centr[...]

By

Tom Cardamone

Herndon, Virginia

Published in the United States
STARbooks Press
PO Box 711612
Herndon VA 20171
Printed in the United States

Many thanks to graphic artist John Nail for the cover design. Mr. Nail may be reached at: tojonail@bellsouth.net.

Book and text design by Milton Stern. Mr. Stern can be reached at miltonstern@miltonstern.com.

Chapter 1. Midnight and After

Burning the ground I break from the crowd.

I'm on the hunt I'm after you.

I smell like I sound, I'm lost and I'm found.

And I'm hungry like the wolf.

– Duran Duran

To the Faery Folk of New Amsterdam daytime Central Park is useless, pedestrian, a simple lawn. Near twilight, a motley group of restless men collect within the Ramble. Men rushing from work, tourists from afar who have long known the legends of the hazardous divinity broached by nightfall, the men who are just somehow always there. After dusk more men gather. Sundown, men shed their shirts, impatiently kicking off boots and shoes, storing them among the worn roots of weary

trees. They begin to shift. They shake out their fingernails into sharp things, arch their backs to a broader, more feral mass, howl as their teeth lengthen. They become wolves, wolves that lean into the dark hovels of trees to open their pants; angry cocks grow under the gaze of the few daring fauns already leaping through the twilight woods. Their cocks seem to breathe, uncoiling from within the dark crouch of new wolves. Naked thighs pulse through ripped, dirty jeans. A glistening new crop of raw, lupine hair pours out.

One werewolf pants as he pushes his cock between the lips of a young, kneeling faun. Inserting a lone claw sharply into the faun's sweaty, proffered rear, the wolf asserts his claim while other wolves circle, some to watch, some likely to charge the scene. Circling, they show each other their teeth, white razors made to rend Faery flesh. The commanding wolf turns his frightened faun around and pushes him to the ground, positioning him on all fours. Firm claws open the boy's backside like a new book. With a low, determined growl, the werewolf forces his solid cock in deep. The internal heat of the faun grips him, and he rears his head back to let loose a howl. This, in turn, spurs the watching werewolves into a frenzy; they pull on their long cocks, biting and nipping at each other. Others roll on their backs to lap at the red cocks of the nearest werewolf, their keen, bright tongues like felty sandpaper.

Wolves put their paws against tall pines and bay at the moon, engorged dicks wavering like potent divining rods powered to charge the night and split many, many fauns. And out come the fauns, skipping lightly over the low stone walls that divide park from city, the click of their lithe, shiny black hooves suddenly muffled by the damp earthen trails leading into the Ramble. Fauns come from distinguished Fifth Avenue shops, where they are gaily employed, dressing windows and folding shirts. Others wait tables in bustling Greenwich Village restaurants, all gossiping together as they prance toward the park. With barely suppressed giggles, they dramatically point toward those human souls hurriedly returning from the Ramble, trailing a shrunken sense of adventure.

Most of these men will likely never return, though among them there are those who will soon thereafter dream wolf-dreams. They will be drawn back in, for they seek not an erotic adventure but an animal destiny. They will return, for them it is not a matter of choice. As the fauns' foray into the Ramble, they adopt a more hushed tone. Holding hands for comfort, they explore the dark twists and turns. Everywhere, wolves in the shadows track their movements, revel in their fresh scent.

The wolf to first claim a faun is done. Turning the young, battered boy over on his back, the wolf pulls his steaming cock out and sprays the leaf-covered form beneath him with wave after wave of viscous seed. As he turns away to focus on fresh prey, the waiting wolves wildly lap up the semen cooling across the faun's heaving chest. The exhausted boy moans lightly, waving his skinny arms in faint protest. They take turns using the faun, stretching him across one of the many large, cold rocks that pepper the Ramble, the surrendered faun weakly licking one wolf cock while being plowed by another.

The night darkens further. More fauns enter the park, and more and more wolves will feed. Midnight will pass. Dawn stains the horizon. Satiated werewolves shimmer back into human shape and wearily retrieve clothes from hidden hovels. Tired, happy fauns abscond from the Ramble. Some will take a refreshing splash through Bethesda Fountain, dipping their rears to leaven the dirt and leaves out of their frazzled coats. They exit nearly content. After returning to their apartments, most will slumber past noon to awake, relishing the evening to come, yearning for that special mercy granted from a bite that does not kill, what lingers far longer than any mortal kiss. The aphrodisiac of absence, jeopardy withheld beneath the moonlight, this is what wholly ignites the Faery soul.

Lycanthropy is transmissible, just not among Faery Folk. Fauns cannot become werewolves – they are only meant to be devoured. True, some fauns skip across the cobblestone only at twilight, never to slink through the bushes after dark, shoulders never whipped by branches as wanton wolves give chase. Such diffident fauns forgo the incomparable indentation of fangs on the slender nape of their sacrificial necks. Some delicate vases prefer not to shatter. So be it. But most take the plunge to join the feast, as is their proper nature.

Of those fauns who emerge to return again and again, almost all will eventually develop into men, their future selves always startled by the memories of their part in the feasts of Central Park, memories seemingly too close to fantasy to be real, excepting that thin, white scar, assumed a birthmark, across a shoulder, a light impression on the underside of a raised arm. Such scars resemble the faintest of bite marks, tactile memories that will draw these men back into the Ramble one evening. A dark revelation awaits those that dare stay; the pleasure so hazily remembered returns as an assault, wounds that last past dawn. Such men return ravaged – filled with the permanent hunger of a werewolf.

After all, nothing is quite as brutal as the past.

Marcus shed the downy blonde coat of faundom not so long ago (or not as long ago as he likes to think). He had wandered out of the park late one morning, actually very late. All fauns go about the city as they would bucolic hills, naked and free. Meaning they don't carry cash, meaning they rely on the kindness of those men so inclined to aid wayward fauns. No such fellows availed themselves to Marcus that morning as he exited the park, making him late to a job where his employment was already less than secure. Cabdrivers are alert to this situation to the point where they won't stop for any faun unaccompanied by the aforementioned gentlemen. Marcus had to jump the turnstile and take the train during rush hour, though he shared the Faery Folk's common aversion to the subway (shades of Hades and all). Commuters stared at him blankly, high school boys pointing and braying as he sat there, the subway seat cold against naked cheeks, greasy from leaking werewolf semen. To add to his delay, upon reaching his building, an absent doorman meant he then had to climb the fire escape and jimmy the window to get into his apartment. Needless to say, he was late for work at the department store. He worked a double-shift to appease management.

That night he went home tired and dejected, breaking, for the first time, his nocturnal ritual of returning to the Ramble every evening – nor did he return the next night. Instead, he

6

went to a bar with the other fauns from work. Together they laughed and drank while around them lurching centaurs kicked up sawdust and glitter from the barroom floor.

That night Marcus kissed another faun, and the spell of the Ramble was broken. Soon after, he lost the fur from his thighs, his hooves dissipated. He became a man. As his nocturnal cravings were redirected, he was able to concentrate on his work, eventually gain a promotion to management, move to a larger apartment, and pick up the cutest boys. The Ramble was a thing of the past, or so he thought. Sometimes after work he would walk past the park and feel the jagged silhouette of the trees menacing him. Shadowy memories arose in his subconscious, lurking near the surface, predatory, a roiling surge of lust he could neither define nor suppress.

Often of late, he awoke parched in his fine, decorous bedroom, thirsty and perturbed over these unremembered dreams, carnal dreams impressed indecipherably upon tapestries ablaze with blinding moonlight.

For Barrett, it was never a matter of choice. The Ramble was destiny. He nearly sprinted toward the park every evening after work, foraging through the brush with a smirk, thinking gamely, "Here the hunter gets captured by the game." Preferring the tall, lone wolves, and not wanting to be the night's

centerpiece for any random feast, Barrett wished to be consumed solely, to experience all of the joy and most of the dread, the pleasure and pain such wild attention merits. As fauns go, Barrett was slender and boyishly short with rare, sprightly chest hair, as curly as the down on his thighs and above his backside, though like other fauns he had no pubic or underarm hair. Often he felt as if he were late getting to the city, late to the park, it had taken him so long to find the nerve to escape his family and small town, so that every night he entered the Ramble with relish, as if this were his last foray in amidst the dark sexual tension, an electric storm of which he was the living center.

Dusk and the last of the tourists made their way from the park while fatigued joggers filtered out of the Ramble. A crease of pink light thinned on the horizon as shadows unfurled. Barely perceptible shifting shapes of men stood against the darkness of the trees. Men walked past him, coming close and staring hard. As his eyes adjusted, he could see the broad, tight chest of a shirtless man leaning against a nearby tree, his features obscured by a low branch. Barrett stood in the path, watching him change. At first, the man did not move, so fully engrossed in the ecstasy of his own transformation, but Barrett could sense the man's muscles tensing, the hair on his arms thickening, the air around him charged. Jeans ripped audibly as

burgeoning thighs expanded. As the change became more pronounced, the man could no longer remain still. He stepped out onto the path, bending down to come at Barrett from behind, sniffing at his exposed ass. The shifting man-wolf tried to force Barrett to the ground, seizing him by the elbow with one strong hand while struggling to free his own wormy, brownish cock with the other. Barrett was not quite ready to partake in the evening's festivities and leapt away. It was too early for a werewolf to land any prey. That was for midnight and after. Both moved on.

Throughout the Ramble, men circled fauns and caressed one another. Now was the time to strip off their clothes and pull on new muscle. One wolf stood nearly invisible within the fold of a massive oak, his huge member shone white and tough as an ancient birch in moonlight, its slight throb pulling Barrett toward the darkness. He was drawn to it, thrilled equally at its commanding size as with the unseen wolf that could possibly rule him with such a magnificent, animal scepter. Instinctively, he knew it was still too early to fully surrender to the Ramble, but the werewolf's cock was hypnotic, tugging Barrett forward, urging him down on his knees. Arms behind him, he knelt and softly caressed the cock with his cheek; ribboned muscle pulsed against his closed, parched lips. He lifted one hand to caress the fur of the werewolf's strong abdomen, the barred gate to an

intense hunger. The wolfman purred approval. This was all Barrett required; opening his mouth wide, he slowly engulfed the thickening cock, swabbing the sticky pre-cum off its ample head with a dexterous tongue. The length and girth of the cock gave him pause. The werewolf bucked hard, driving his face in anger at having been denied for even that one second. Barrett felt another beast scratch at his anus but petulantly swatted the errant paw away. He wanted to focus solely on this beautiful cock. He wanted to serve.

The wolf in his mouth grunted, allowing his long nails to brush back and forth across Barrett's scalp like an ominous pendulum. His mouth was open as wide as possible and still he could barely contain the massive cock pummeling his throat. The werewolf was still for a moment. The faun froze. The long cock lay in his mouth like dormant lightning then withdrew. The wolf turned his back to Barrett, lupine skull cocked to the wind, the scent of another distant faun percolating in his enflamed nostrils. He bounded off into the night.

Barrett stood and brushed the leaves from his elbows and buttocks. He was not offended. It was too early for either of them to climax. This was simply the way the night began. They might even meet again, among other shadows. The werewolf might take him from behind after chasing him across the Great

Lawn. Not recognizing each other, Barrett would perform the same ritual. Or not. Regardless, both made their way through the Ramble, having warmed to any encounter, primed to take it to the next level.

Around the corner, another faun was struggling in the arms of a massive werewolf, one with a gray coat and sharp, long ears. Barrett could see his teeth gleaming in the moonlight, a dangerous array of wicked diamonds; the faun's tear-filled eyes also glimmered, with the sparkle of an equally multi-faceted fear. Two more wolves emerged to snatch at the faun, each hoisting a leg as if the boy were a mere wishbone. A fourth werewolf lopped out from the darkness to kneel beneath the now raised faun, sniffing curiously at the faun's exposed, ripe ass. He licked it with his large, harsh tongue before inserting one of his claws. The faun let out a whimper, but his struggling subsided. With this surrender, the wolves began to howl, the gray wolf turning him over so the others could take turns mounting him. Torn from the earth, now afloat, one rough cock after another entering his every orifice, the faun's torso shook, a plank of ecstasy. The werewolves panted and drooled. Those at the faun's arms held him aloft with one strong claw while stroking one another's elongated, red cocks. Barrett swiftly and quietly moved away before he was forced to join. These early fauns were better off keeping to the shadows rather than openly

cruising. To get bitten or raped too soon would spoil the night, though certainly there were numerous fauns not so delicate as to endure multiple encounters. Many more savored that dark, tasty fear, the anticipation of a midnight chase.

Barrett could make out the naked pale shoulders of several fauns hidden in the brush, baiting temptation. His own erection from his earlier encounter was lessening; the head of his cock withdrew into the fair sheath of his foreskin. He turned a corner that lead to a high stone bridge and paused. An ebony werewolf stood panting beneath the dim lamp post that illuminated the arch of the bridge. The black wolf glistened with sweat – his hair matted and pearled with moisture. He stood beneath the light with his legs spread wide, his hard black cock like the needle of a powerful compass quivering toward one direction: Barrett. And Barrett could tell the werewolf had recently given chase to a faun and likely let him escape, prolonging the night, sweetening the eventual capture of any prey. With fiery eyes, the dark wolf gave him a commanding look. Barrett obediently dropped to his knees. With a quick, assured stride, the werewolf was upon him, mounting his mouth with an animal growl. He gasped for air as the wolf's wide cock routed his mouth in one long, deep plunge. He nearly choked on the sinewy pre-cum caulking the back of his throat. Rather than struggle, he clasped the hairy calves of the werewolf to steady

himself. He fed slavishly, working his tongue beneath the thick canvas of foreskin billowing into his mouth. The werewolf paused, and Barrett braced himself for the wave of thick semen surely about to flood his mouth. The beast had other plans; with cock still firmly planted in suppliant mouth, he turned his attention toward a trembling faun half hidden beside a tree at the other side of the bridge. With the same commanding stare with which he summoned Barrett, the werewolf demanded the faun approach. In the stark light of the lamp post, the faun appeared scared and frail, considerably smaller than Barrett, a youthful creature whose curly black locks were shorn just short enough to reveal the silver cut of elfin ears. His slender waist tapered into boney, hairless hips from which sprouted a small, hardy penis – the hair on his thighs, the thick, white coat of a faun just past adolescence. The frightened creature began to lower himself, mouth open, to replicate the service offered by Barrett. The wolf let out such an angry roar leaves shook loose from the trees. The boys shivered in fear. The impatient wolf turned and put one huge claw atop the young faun's head, directing him to kneel and please Barrett.

With renewed vigor, the werewolf continued plundering Barrett's mouth, his pendulous testicles stirring the little faun's sweaty hair as the boy tenderly took Barrett's cock between his own tremulous lips. He winced as the tiny, amateur teeth raked

13

the thickening flesh of his cock, though he was careful not to lose his rhythm, lest he suffer the werewolf's wrath. The monster howled, struggling to push his cock impossibly deeper into Barrett's mouth. Barrett was nearly faint from such an infusion of sensation; tears streaking down his cheeks further seasoned his pain while pleasure rose from the meek faun nibbling at his cock like a sweet, docile lamb. But such is the erratic nature of encounters in the Ramble; just as Barrett adjusted to his new partner and his momentary master's renewed thrusting, his lamb-like servant was suddenly yanked away with a cry. The werewolf turned sharply, jerking his cock out from between Barrett's startled lips, knocking him to the ground where all he could see was the wide-eyed faun on his back, impossibly large claws clasped around his tiny ankles, pulling him into the dark foliage. The werewolf bounded after the stolen faun, as likely as not to fight with the other wolf or pair up for a dual assault.

Barrett found himself alone and starkly vulnerable, breathing heavily, his heart racing, one cheek smeared with saliva and glutinous semen. His hard cock was still moist from the diminutive faun's attention; he scooped up some of the faun's spittle from his twitching member and licked his finger. Tasting the sad sugar of innocence, he stood and brushed himself off. He heard distant whimpering from the bushes, the

grunting of wolves. The hour was now late – the hunt had begun in earnest. The pain of need tightened in Barrett's chest. He must find a werewolf to serve, the right beast to savagely shred his desire.

As he crossed the bridge, his shadow clung desperately to the base of the lamp post, mingling with the inky remnants of previous passing shadows, reveling in the homey comfort of new black scents before being yanked like an errant pet back into the greater darkness of the night.

Chapter 2. Faery Folk

I never came back home with quite the same moral character I went out with.

– Seneca

Oh, how Marcus liked the taste of fauns, lifting cinnamon kisses from their lips, often comparing their soft hesitancy night-to-night, their nervous breath sustaining him more than his own. He found centaurs annoying, however, and wished the better fauns would congregate somewhere other than Stables, a Faery Folk bar renowned for quick cruising and cheap ambrosia. Whenever he picked up a trick at Stables, the inevitable sawdust soiled his sheets in the morning, much to his annoyance. He never drank enough ambrosia to turn centaur, so certainly he did not despise them as other men do, fearful that

this was their own gross future, the result of their vices galloping away. Marcus had very few vices; just kissing fauns, bedding them, sending them off at dawn while he dressed for work. Lately though, this had not been enough. A mild discordance colored everything. He had a comfortable career, a fine apartment. The best of fauns were attracted to him. Yet, even now, his thoughts drifted back toward his walk home this evening, the dark allure of the park at sundown.

A cute boy entered the bar. The faun looked new to the city, wearing a fresh, red polo shirt with the collar up, bare below the waist, of course (the natural predilection of all fauns) – small, svelte cock buoyant above the plush hair of his thighs, his slight hooves shone of fresh black polish atop the dusty floor. As the new faun surveyed the bar, he casually ran his fingers through a mass of curly blonde hair. Marcus admired the tight and proper musculature of the perfect arm and was surprised to see that he was wearing a watch, loose on a gold chain, a daring fashion statement as most Faery Folk are allergic to Time. The faun had a slight but sharp chin and a decidedly masculine brow.

Marcus decided to forget his undefined troubles. He must have this faun. First, he established polite yet firm eye-contact. It was important to discern early on whether he was a

filly-chaser, one of those unfathomable fauns who preferred, though it really was beyond Marcus's comprehension, the company of centaurs. He respected and even appreciated those fauns who sought out each other's company – how he enjoyed the challenge of enticing them both back to his bed. But the boy in the red shirt confidently returned his smile. He motioned him over and ordered another cup of ambrosia. The bartender was a rather youngish centaur with a noble bearing and palomino complexion, his brevity of conversation greatly appreciated by Marcus. As the young faun approached, he offered his hand by way of introduction, holding the boy's hand longer than formality dictates, to better gauge the young faun's shyness. The boy's small hand fit warmly in his.

"I'm Christopher." His smile was intoxicating.

Marcus offered him a fresh cup of frothy ambrosia; the preferred drink among Faery Folk and often their admirers, as if the mere taste was an introductory force into their secret worlds. Well, for those who imbibed too much, it was. He barely tolerated the taste himself. For humans, it was a drink with consequence. While continuing to hold his hand close, Marcus placed his other hand warmly on the boy's shoulder, asking that preliminary question that politely launches all initial, New

Amsterdam conversations. "So, how long have you been in the city?"

His answer was sweet and, for Marcus, blessedly short. He casually released his grip on the boy and took a short sip from his drink.

For the second act of his seduction, Marcus looked around the room, giving the boy an opportunity to both admire him as well as realize that he was confident enough to still fish about with his eyes. Usually this had young fauns quickly bleating for attention, and when he returned their gaze they always looked so grateful, grateful and willing.

It was near midnight, and the bar was full. Several centaurs had already passed out in corner booths, their snores kept time with the soft disco beats drifting from the jukebox. A bevy of fauns danced together in the center of the room while lecherous centaurs leering from the bar did their best to tuck their erections between their legs; occasionally the heads of their bright pink cocks could be seen eagerly wagging away.

Bill was one of these centaurs. No matter how long he had been a centaur, he would never get used to how rapidly his dick extended at the mere sight of a cute faun. Worse were those who took torturous delight in this incidental arousal. "Oh

my sir, it's so big!" "Is that on my account?" "Oh my, Mr. Centaur, might I touch it?" Such nonsense gave his by-then-rock-hard cock cause to just drool pre-cum, twitching for a chance to explore the offending ripe, likely virginal (or so he always imagined) buttocks.

He observed a handsome man at the bar talking to the new faun who had just entered. Seeing how the man gingerly fingered the spike of the boy's nipple though his neat shirt gave such an ache to his penis that he had to look away.

The curse of being a centaur is not the clumsy form, he thought, nor the disrespect granted by their size, the fondness for liquor that's all consuming, but that their horse-half is so entirely out of the reach of their all-too-human hands!

All those years ago, when Bill awoke with what he expected to be the mother of all hangovers, only to discover he was heavy, distorted, beyond all imagination a lumbering centaur upon a paltry, crushed bed frame. Horror tinged by mild erotic curiosity as he noticed, while lying on his side, that his new member was proudly emerging at just over two feet in length. This gorgeous crimson plaything would have made the transformation somewhat endurable if only he could reach it! What cruelty of nature would keep him from his own cock? But nature did not make these rules. The trouble with living in an

enchanted city is the enchantment itself, always something serpentine, invisible, wound tight among the city spires, lending the heft of its radiance to New Amsterdam. Mere citizens bask in its brilliance, and where one lone scale can incidentally shield you from a twisted warlock's spell, the very next day, still bedazzled by your fortune, a flick of the tail, and you are fully pierced by magic's fang, transformed by vinegary barb into wolf or centaur.

Too much ambrosia makes a man turn centaur. Bill long ago worked past lamenting his four-legged form. Every enchantment seems a curse until you know better. Among the Faery Folk, only centaurs incite their transformation solely via drink – lots and lots of drink. And achieving fantastic animal form is not the last stop. If too much ambrosia makes a man turn centaur, too much more turns a centaur beast. More ambrosia, as if waking up half horse wasn't a call for recourse, a bit of self-examination and possibly a realignment of habit. No, the resulting fury and confusion, the bitter disappointment, the inevitable likelihood of lost employment, embarrassed and suddenly receding friendships, all lead to more drinking. And you can still drink too much, drink past the last of your humanity. Drink yourself mad. Such coarsened centaurs know only one fate: corralled behind a chain-link fence at the grim, grassy stables of Idlewild. Exiled on the outskirts of JFK's

longest runway, herds of centaur howl, smeared with their own excrement, stampeding beneath the metallic bellies of impassive jets swooping over their mad heads. Either landing or departing, the foaming beasts wave their gnarled, cracked hands toward every passing plane, desperate but forever unable to grapple with something larger than themselves.

Bill decided to forgo another drink. All around, fauns flirted with one another, approaching the bar only long enough for a drunken centaur to buy them a drink. Bill knew that by now those who frequented the Ramble had already skipped off to the park, that some of these remaining fauns might just prefer him. But which ones? Those fauns that dare take on a centaur are the most circumspect, as centaurs are contentious drunks and thus dangerous lovers. These thoughts strained his dick even more. Embarrassed that he might actually cum then and there on the floor, as had, sadly, happened to him in the past, he quickly downed the last drop of ambrosia from his cup in one quick gulp and galloped toward the exit, concerned less with the dust he kicked up than the rigid loneliness between his legs that followed him like a determined arrow wherever he went.

As a centaur rudely barreled past, Marcus shielded the faun with his arm, pulling him closer.

"They're terrible this time of night. Would you like to go somewhere else?" he asked Christopher.

"Sure, how about your place?"

The boy replied with a nubile confidence, looking up at him with large, brown eyes. Marcus cupped Christopher's head in his hands and gently kissed him. First, he just touched his tongue to the boy's parting lips, and then leaned in until his bottom lip grated across Christopher's sharp chin; he then pulled the faun's head back and consumed his neck. The faun held his waist tightly – Marcus let one hand drop to grasp the boy's hard little prick. He placed Christopher's hand on the ample swelling within the crotch of his jeans. The song from the jukebox ended as they headed for the door.

At his apartment, Marcus undressed before his faun. He sensed that this was the boy's first time, so he disrobed slowly, leaving the lights on. Christopher kneeled before him, mouth agape and eyes wide, totally transfixed. Marcus shed his clothes with a graceful nonchalance that best exhibited his natural musculature, his thick arms and broad chest. The patch of dark pubic hair bonded to his pelvis hypnotized the faun. He stood as still as a statue while Christopher reverently inspected him, stooping to deeply inhale the rich forestry of odor wafting from

his crotch. His breath on Marcus' cock had the natural effect. As his dick thickened and grew, he led Christopher to the bed and made him lie down on his stomach. Obediently, the faun complied, placing one hand between his legs and balled the other in a fist beneath his forehead, elbow out. Marcus gently parted the boy's lithe legs to better view the tight swirl of his virginity. Spreading his full cheeks wide for a closer inspection, using his thumbs to stretch it taunt, Marcus leaned in and briefly let his tongue flicker across the faun's fractured pink nugget.

A new sense of rapture raced up the boy's back – his entire body shook; he pushed his ass up in the air, physically begging for more. Marcus paused. With one hand still holding the boy's hole open he spit in his other hand and kneaded his throbbing cock. He thought better of entering the boy so suddenly, though every ounce of his soul begged for just that. He calmly licked one of his fingers, and with great patience, unlocked his secret, exposing a warm promise of more.

Bleating, Christopher furiously tugged at his little penis. With a calming assurance, Marcus pulled the boy's hand out from under him, least he climax too soon – finger all the way in, turning like a volcanic key to prepare the boy, ensure the coming shock would overwhelm but not harm. When he withdrew, Christopher gasped. Again, he spit in his hand and

further lubed his cock. Placing his other hand firmly on the back of his slender neck to assert control, Marcus rested the barrel of his cock within the boy's sweaty groove. With a single, terrific thrust, he launched himself inward, tunneling deep into unconquered flesh. Christopher pushed himself further into the mattress, body rebelling against desire, as if he could douse the kindling of his spirit. To keep from crying out, he bit his fist. Eyes closed, Marcus thrust deeper, moving from side to side as Christopher twitched and wailed beneath him. Beneath him, but somehow splashing up around him, their mutual heat enveloped them both. Marcus felt as if he were climbing a steaming waterfall, impossibly trying to ford the River of Boy. A journey toward drowning, the mouth of exaltation a sea of sweat and tears hemmed by rising, salty waves, two foamy lips about to clash.

As he saddled the boy with his tumescent cock, sweat dripped from his forehead, stung his eyes. Striking the faun's back, it streaked downward to further moisten his battered hole. He leaned further into the boy's curved form and straightened out both arms. Clutching at the damp sheets, he arched his back. Goatish hooves swam vainly in the air. Marcus opened his mouth like a man parched as the sea poured out.

He collapsed along side the faun. The boy rolled over, dazed and shaking. His body literally hummed. Panting, Christopher lay there, his eyes shone like black opals, potent treasure excavated from the sands of a desert that covered the world, a treasure unclaimed and uncursed, ageless and new. His body convulsed rhythmically, slowing slightly, a gold rivulet leaking from the sharp point of his cock, blotting the hovel of his firm stomach with luminescent islands, each reaching toward the other as his breathing calmed.

When Marcus returned from the shower, Christopher was still on his back, deep in slumber, dreaming his first dreams of men from memory, and not veiled fantasy. Marcus observed the boy while toweling himself and noticed the little pockets of semen congealing on his stomach, painting the overturned starfish of his bellybutton silver and yellow. The stuff of comets, he thought. Carefully, he lay beside the boy's peaceful body and dove for the rich harvest. After lapping up the more accessible drops, he used his fingernail to surgically lift the last hardening pearl from within the shallow folds of the faun's silken foreskin.

When Marcus wakes in the morning, he will likely smile at the soft, shallow valley the boy will leave in his bed and

think, "How like a faun. They do like to sneak out in the middle of the night."

While drifting off to sleep, he sucked at the bitterness between his teeth.

Chapter 3. There Is a Light That Never Goes Out

If you are looking for love

In a looking glass world,

It's pretty hard to find

– Roxy Music

Myth: Werewolves can take and keep their shape only within the confines of Central Park. False, though this is something many werewolves themselves are not even aware of.

However, lycanthropy unique to Central Park cannot be spread or transmitted beyond the park. Take a pixie's eye-view of the phenomenon, and you would see that the lycanthropy particular to New Amsterdam is almost wholly confined to the rather limited area of the Ramble, a hilly area, a jumble of paths

the radius of a few city blocks. This pinprick of feral arcadia is dead center Central Park, roughly demarcated by Bow Bridge just above Bethesda Fountain, ending at the Seventy-Ninth Street Transverse to the north. A moody pond buffers the Ramble on the West side, while to the East, the boathouse and subsequent footpath provide natural boundaries. And though the very nature of night deludes all boundaries, this is not the point. The confines of the Ramble are not a guarantee but more a natural restriction placed by the werewolves upon themselves.

In a city of men, wolves would be more than conspicuous, they would be hunted. The rich ignore this rule as they ignore so many others. And of course, rich wolves hunt in packs. What good would such powers be if unobserved by peers? Such wolves, disdainful of the Ramble, meet in high-rise lofts, private apartments, having formed perverse supper clubs for such rendezvous, focusing on the youngest of the fauns, rewarding them handsomely for the right to be devoured in such a voluptuous manner. These dark gatherings are what wolves and fauns refer to as a Banquet.

Barrett lay on the couch recalling the last Banquet he had attended. He had been relieved to discover the event was not nearly as violent as rumored, but still the experiences therein were harrowing, experiences for which he and his

roommate had been handsomely rewarded. The secret is to stick to one wolf the whole night, his more experienced roommate, Hector, had counseled. Pick one with a bit of silver in his mane and a penchant for wine. It's not like the Ramble. These werewolves are more possessive and more willing to take their time. It's the fauns who are alone after midnight who are devoured, so to speak. You stick with the one that fancies you the most, and you'll be fine. After all, the rich have a way of raping you that makes you almost want to thank them.

He had said this with a wink, turning his head just so, to better accentuate the large diamond earring, plucked from the paws of a silver wolf after the last Banquet he attended, and Hector had attended a lot of Banquets.

Still, he warned, not every faun was so lucky. At every Banquet, someone is the main course.

Fauns are notoriously late sleepers, loving nothing more than a good, long nap. And Barrett had slept past noon, meaning he had slept himself out of a job. He napped around the apartment all day, waiting for Hector to come home. Hazily, he recalled hearing their new roommate, Christopher, returning just before dawn, easing the heavy door shut behind him. Again and again, his thoughts drifted back to his first nocturnal trips to the Ramble, the exhilaration of his initial foraging in the bars. The

experiences that awaited the still sleeping Christopher were an initiation like no other. From the shabby couch, long ago rescued from the curb, to the mismatched and often chipped china piled precariously in the sink, Barrett knew that no matter how cozy their apartment was, at best it was a make-shift home. The building was full of traipsing fauns who would some day become men. And how soon it would happen to Hector – the thought had secretly worried Barrett for some time. That was one experience he did not thirst for and likely Christopher had yet to really entertain.

Crossing his legs, Barrett licked his thumb and shined the hoof bobbing before him. Hector will be upset that he lost his job. Still, it was good impetus for Hector to get them invited to the next Banquet.

Bill woke up with the prerequisite hangover. Fortunately, his Greenwich Village apartment was on a quiet side street. Wafting through the open window, pre-autumn breeze and birdsong soothed his splitting head. He made a breakfast of strong coffee, black, and a bowl of oats, wishing he had slept longer, having nothing really to do until Stables opened for happy hour. He surveyed his apartment: a knot of worn pillows, no furniture of worth, just piles of books, loose pages everywhere from books that had slid from the safety of

their stack, accidentally trampled by drunken hooves in the night. He was fortunate to have been in the building nearly two decades, meaning he benefited from ridiculously low, controlled rent as well as simple good luck. When he was first struck with centaurism, a neighbor had traded apartments with him so he could be on the ground floor, stairs being impossible to navigate. Traded? More like a friendly act of piracy, as he relinquished a one-bedroom apartment with vaulted ceilings for a studio that felt rather cramped to a man half horse. Well, as necessity dictates. He was one of the lucky ones, able to parlay his former job as a corporate accountant into a part-time thing, setting up a card table in Washington Square during the warmer days of early spring. Doing taxes for Faery Folk and curious college students, charging less than his store-front competitors, had kept him from poverty, but two months' work is a hard way to pay a year's worth of rent. Still, he counted himself fortunate. Most centaurs pull carriages in Central Park at terrible wages or scrap together a meager subsistence from a variety of charitable and governmental sources.

The book he was currently reading rested respectfully atop an antique music stand, a gift from a true friend, as most centaurs prefer to read standing up. The current page was marked by a yellowed antique post card, a black and white reproduction of an even earlier daguerreotype of a pert little

pixie in mid-curtsey. Bill stood and thought about pixie friends long gone; the dull pain of his hangover lurched toward sadness. Not so long after the War, when he first moved to the city as a young man, pixies were still quite common, one of the more established and accepted Faery Folk in New Amsterdam. Over the years, as their collective glow slowly extinguished, Bill felt that more than just a little of the city's magic was lost as well. Tiny living lights had graced New Amsterdam generations before the full exodus of Faery Folk from the forests of the Old World, tiny living lights blinking out, one by one, a galaxy of delicate spirits, gone. Stars in the palm of your hand, they would light your cigarette with the snap of a wingtip, all gone. They had crossed with the original Dutch settlers, merrily lighting street lamps (this was before gas, before electricity, back when all of New Amsterdam clustered around a single church below Canal Street, back when Canal Street was in actuality a canal, putrid from human sewage and the occasional dead livestock). Pixies lit the city, and when the city outgrew them, they lit Broadway, enchanted running boards for plays and musicals.

Bill was no fan of werewolves, after all they thought of him as nothing more than a steak on legs, but clearly the blame, at least partially, lay rightly with them. Soldiers returning from the War in Europe brought lycanthropy to Central Park, taking

up nocturnal residence in the Ramble, wherein the last lamps lit by pixie-light also formed their sole habitat. As fauns immigrated to the city, they naturally took to the pastoral majesty of the park and made perfect friends to the pixies. But to the werewolves, pixies were an annoying illumination to their trysts, that and a quick snack. Their flight from the park was their downfall. They had to live among men, men who did not appreciate their previous service to think beyond plucking their wings, sold as souvenirs: Membranous bookmarks and laminated key chains, horrible plastic goodbyes.

He picked up the post card and reviewed the canceled postage on the back. The hushed reverence toward Faery Folk had long passed. Electricity, atomic bombs and astronauts, the feats of mortal men rendered the enchanted quaint. The Faery Folk were now living antiquities. Just last month, he had passed the entrance of a reputable bookstore, its haughty door held ajar by the large, chalky skull of a Cyclops, a black cat napping in the hollow of its orbicular cave. Imagine. It was as if the kinetic events of the last century reduced previous centuries to ash – among the ash, Faery dust. He gently closed the book on the music stand, thinking the pixie-postcard seemed somehow resolute, tattered and old yet still retaining a unique luster, the last note to a song sad but forever true.

Tom Cardamone

Chapter 4. A Faun in Central Park

I made it through the wilderness.

– Madonna

Christopher was about to make his first foray into the Ramble. He slipped out of the apartment while Barrett and Hector conspired in the kitchen. After pilfering an apple from a street vender in Union Square, he leisurely strolled up Broadway as the sun set a florid cherry fan down across the horizon. Reaching the park as the sky finally darkened, he hopped the low cobblestone fence bordering Central Park West and stood still among the nearest trees, their shadows wrapping around his ankles, enticing him further toward mystery. He knew the general direction from the gossip of other fauns and set off on the winding path as the park's lamp posts flickered to

life, dim stationary fireflies held by rusty tethers, their low, constant electric rumble adding to the menace permeating the air. He knew that once he crossed either Bow Bridge or found the path above the boat basin, he would enter the Ramble. A slight dread tightened in his chest. As the chill coming off the pond crept into the freshly-brushed pelt of his thighs, he stepped into the plaza woven around Bethesda Fountain. The moon's nimbus stung the clouds into bits of floating charcoal. The lilting laughter of unseen fauns in the distance comforted him. It was still too early for wolves to bay.

Steeling himself, he sprinted over the bridge. Almost immediately, he felt a difference, a sexual energy, a tangible addition to the multiple layers of shadow expanding with dusk. Men stood within the thicket. He could not make out their faces, but he knew he was being observed. "I'm here!" Christopher thought, exuberant, frightened and aroused. He felt the initial twitch of an erection and decided to trot further down the path, deeper into the woods, worried that his budding arousal would prematurely attract attention – he wanted the night to last.

Since entering faunhood, he had entertained wild fantasies of sacrifice, invisible beasts tearing at him through impossible fields of darkness, biting his neck while ravaging his backside. Many a night he would wake up from such dreams

panting heavily, long tendrils of semen splayed between his belly and thighs.

As he moved among the trees, he sensed that the men within were changing. Beside the trunk of one massive gnarled oak, a man squatted on all fours, having shed all his clothes. Christopher watched the man shiver in delight as strands of hair coursed across his shoulder blades. In the moonlight, he could see the man's emerging claws push into the earth, his penis swinging heavy between his legs, the moist, angry head rolling out of his foreskin like a blind, subterranean animal. Hypnotized by this transformation, the spell suddenly broke as the werewolf returned his gaze with a primordial lust, eyes narrowing into silver canine mirrors reflecting an indifferent moon. Christopher backed up slowly and took off down the path, his heart racing, the wand of his tiny hardening cock slapping against his thighs.

He ran past shifting shapes, men groped wolves as they themselves sprouted new, black manes and long, sharp teeth. He nearly bolted over the bridge and out of the Ramble but paused. The edge of the park was in view, the neat silhouette of skyscrapers hovering far above the waving trees behind him. Should he part the curtain and entertain the feast? The Feast. The Sacrifice. Shivering, he held himself, feeling his slender bones beneath gooseflesh, imagining them snapping like twigs

in the hanging jaws of some wolf gone mad. Christopher was startled as two frolicking fauns skipped past. Their titled heads drew close in whispering, effervescent gossip, one faun with fur so white it shone silver in the moonlight, the other a complexion of rich chocolate, a fine, shaggy coat ending in a nimble, upright little tail. Hand-in-hand, they were swallowed by the Ramble. The black vacuum of their sudden arrival and departure left him cold. Then, instinctively, he knew. This was his true invitation. For after the feast as well as before, there would only be darkness. Leaping back down the path, Christopher knew that tonight he belonged to the Ramble.

Immersed in shadow, Christopher wound through the twisting paths. He tried to surrender to the sounds of the Ramble, the primordial grunts and sighs of interlocked werewolf and faun. This song should be mine, he thought. Yet with every howl, fear turned in his chest; the sharp, terrified bleat of a far-off faun unnerved him, the park's melodies of pain had not yet turned to pleasure, the symphony was still in rehearsal, the broken cacophony of which terrorized a naive Christopher. With each twist of the path, his natural sense of direction, so innately unerring among fauns, became more and more dilute, compounded by the darkness of the park at night.

At some point, while winding through the thicket, fearful for every sound, he realized he was being followed. Every time he turned around, the pursuant wolf receded stealthily into shadow. Heart trembling, he quickened his pace through the woods. He was surprised to find he was as equally terrified as aroused. As he ran, a slim strand of silvery pre-cum undulated between the tip of his bobbing cock and stomach. He imagined sharp claws reaching for him, pulling him down, but every time he turned around his stalking shade spun from view. And a new horror forcefully bloomed within his heart. "What if I am being pursued by Bane?"

The Ramble, by its very nature, is synonymous with anonymity, with one exception. Bane. The werewolf Bane's legacy of brutality spread beyond the usually circumspect world of the Ramble to become the stuff of legend city-wide, dark tales repeated in hushed whispers at the bars, tales of formidable wolves torn from their fauns and plundered, sightings of Bane at dawn. Still defiantly in full wolf-form as other men, tired and satiated slinked away back to their apartments and desk jobs, there roared Bane straddling the highest rock, ruefully howling down the sun, angrily waving away gnats with the gnawed thighbone of a freshly devoured faun. Bane, recognized first by his volcanic red eyes, then his bludgeon-cock, a cock so big, so

menacing that Christopher heard one drunken centaur tell of it, "We should give that monster it's own name as well."

Regret washed over Christopher. He regretted coming here, letting thin fantasies dictate his actions. He saw why those silly boys at Stables cuddled up to all of those lumbering, predictable, harmless, hiccupping centaurs. Frantically, he wanted out.

As he increased his pace to a mad rush through the Ramble, he heard a force crashing through the woods behind him. His pursuer abandoned all animal furtiveness. Howling gleefully, he raked the lower branches above the path with his extended, welcoming claws. Panicked, Christopher felt hot breath singe the back of his neck. The edge of the park was within sight. Pushing through the thicket, Christopher was at full speed, drenched in sweat, yet he felt that the breath warming his neck was even, measured. The wolf at his back was keeping pace with him without strain, could in fact catch Christopher if desired. He hesitated in his sprint, rocking back ever so slightly on one hoof until he was engulfed by strong arms, the breath warming his neck turned into a hot bite, bringing him down roughly onto the cobblestone path.

Shocked by the impact, Christopher found himself spun on his back by commanding, sure claws. He looked up into the face of a young werewolf, his features nearly human. Towering over the boy, the wolf cut a lean form with a tapered waist almost as thin as a faun's, though a wide, triangular chest poured forth, bursting with wiry dark hair. An equally black mane hung low over his lupine brow, nearly obscuring intense, fiery eyes aglow from the chase. Thick lips parted to reveal slight fangs. Above the tight knot of testicles swathed in unruly black hair, a perfect cock arched forward between his legs, completely engorged, throbbing in unison with the wolf's every breath. The werewolf held him in his gaze, savoring the scent of his fear and arousal. Bravely, Christopher reached up and slowly ran his fingers through the mat of hair across the werewolf's broad chest; the young creature arched his back and howled. Throughout the Ramble, a loose chorus of howls arose, congratulating the young buck on his first hunt, spurring him on to feast.

In response, the werewolf pushed the young faun's knees up to his chest to reveal a sliver of pink innocence. With a firm grip, he widened the exposure, charting this border of hot flesh with one knife-like claw. Christopher closed his eyes, gasping in pleasure, his body riveted by this initial touch, his

very soul sure in this exploration, imploring the wolf to go further, to enter him and make him whole.

The quivering faun felt a rumbling growl build within the werewolf, like a train about to derail. He tensed his every muscle for the moment of entry. And it came. It came so sharp and forcefully, Christopher let out a cry, his hands clutching madly at the cool earth. Wonderful pain spread through him, internal lightning rocketing through his entire form, from his taunt calves to his rapid heart, sensation struck every molecule. The wolf chorus arose anew, louder now, guttural applause at their sweaty coupling in the dirt. The young werewolf rode him expertly, each thrust deep, commanding. Christopher felt his body welcome the invasion. As he collapsed beneath the momentum of such a well-driven cock, he reached down to finger his own dick, as hard and alabaster as freshly chiseled marble. Slowing their friction, the werewolf leaned in to set the low growl of satisfaction in the faun's ear. He ran his coarse tongue up and down the faun's vulnerable neck. Christopher, eyes tightly shut, parted his lips in a silent plea for a kiss. Sudden hot breath filled his mouth. He sighed in ecstasy – thick, steeping hot goo flowed out of his nimble cock, milky strings struck his bent abdomen as the werewolf broke from their kiss.

Arching his back, the wolf burrowed deeper for the final assault. Bracing himself above the boy, eyes lost to the dark sky, feral lips parted, load after load of wolf semen pulsed into the boy's strained, slippery funnel. He howled at the moon. Tears ran down Christopher's face. The panting werewolf leaned forward and gave him a penetrating look, one of total contentment, then playfully dove down to lap up the acrid cream cooling on his belly, wolf cock still fully inside the boy, retracting ever so slightly, softening in the warmth between them.

Chapter 5. The Underworld

Fairies are a pale and motley race that flowers in the minds of decent folk. Never will they be entitled to broad daylight, to real sun. But, remote in these limbos, they cause curious disasters, which are harbingers of new beauties.

– Jean Genet

Marcus had been at Stables all night drinking and cruising, hoping to catch a glimpse of the faun he had scored with the night before. Unused to an attraction that lasted past dawn, he felt uneasy and was drinking more than usual. Unable to connect with any of the boys currently at the bar, he thought about ordering another drink then cautioned himself. "Easy boy, too many of these, and you'll turn into a centaur." He pulled his

ragged-but-loved baseball cap down over his eyes. He retrieved his leather jacket from coat check and walked out into the night.

The street was noisy and crowded with tourists and revelers. For some reason, they further darkened his mood. He stood on the corner trying to decide just what it was he wanted tonight. Too early to go home, he wanted a boy, but the effort was beyond him. And that settled it. A devilish smile struck across his face. Only one place to go, he told himself – Pluto's Basement.

Pluto's Basement, nearly the last of the old Faery bars in Times Square. Dank, cavernous and marvelously simple: drinking upstairs, fucking downstairs. Nobody went home with anybody. Every transaction, no matter how hot and heavy, took place there in the nooks and corners of the basement. Marcus felt his cock stiffening in his jeans as he stepped into the street, impatiently waving down a cab.

The ride uptown was maddeningly slow. Traffic slithered with an indifference measured by glaring red lights and rude horns. Eventually, he threw some crumpled bills at the driver and walked the last few blocks.

Pluto's was situated on the outskirts of the theater district, where neon lights and tony restaurants surrendered their

legendary streets to tired little cafes and weary bodegas tucked beneath torn awnings, and hidden among them, bars, windows painted black, festered as well. Among the hobbled survivors of the once-thriving decadence of Times Square, Pluto's Basement alone endured by a reptilian brilliance, an unvanquished toxicity that quite possibly could only be extinguished by burning the entire block to the ground. It would be wrong, though, to equate Pluto's to some sort of spiritual cavity. If anything, the sacred was here in excess, the sacredness of sacrifice. Such an establishment did not survive on need alone. No, Pluto himself was in residence most nights. The only God to reside fulltime in New Amsterdam (most having settled in Florida, a few still clinging to Greece as if the past were a soon-to-return lifeboat, Mount Olympus a grand ocean liner hogging the horizon, and not dusted by smog, harangued by tourist laden helicopters … where's a thunderbolt when you need one?).

Well, sans Olympus, sans Boca Raton, sans penthouse, Pluto never left his basement, his skin was deep cobalt, as if lacking heaven he secreted the very hue of his eviction. Completely bald, another refutation – locks shorn to physically disavow any resemblance to Zeus, paterfamilias and banishing brother, though both favored the same Italian designer sunglasses. All Gods wear sunglasses. Marcus didn't know why, but surmised that the various deities on earth likely wished

49

OK here:

to shield us from the obvious pity in their eyes, pity that we are mortal. Pity or utter indifference.

He pushed the unmarked door open and stared steadily into the stony eyes of the large, gray-skinned bouncer, the infamous Janus. The bouncer's most formidable attribute, what made him indispensable to his trade, was that he was literally two-faced, with eyes in the back of his head. He had twin mouths, dour and thin-lipped, two pug noses, each gripping a rueful pair of teardrop-like nostrils. Both sets of eyes were cold, as impenetrable as smoky quartz. Janus returned his gaze and with a bored shrug stepped aside.

Inside, Marcus shoved money under the small frosted window of the ticket booth, from which an elderly woman's skeletal hand emerged slowly to point toward a heavy curtain. The entrance fee was a pittance, but a special woe greeted those who did not pay. After all, Pluto craved guests, so much so that the cover charge did not so much grant entry as guarantee exit. Marcus could not repress a shudder, a mixture of anticipation and dread. Parting a velvet curtain so frequently drawn its luster had thinned to the uncomfortably smooth felt of dead flesh, he quickly bypassed coat check, clogged as it was with greenish slack-jawed trolls grumbling over having to tender their bulky clubs.

50

His eyes adjusted to the darkness. Small, red candles pocked the internal night of Pluto's, momentarily snuffed by figures crossing the small, cramped room. Men huddled over their drinks at the bar, others milled about in the middle of the room, some trying to build up the courage to plunge into the cavernous basement, others deliberately nursing their drinks, hoping to regain enough stamina to return again and again to the sexual apocalypse unfolding downstairs.

That the narrow stairwell leading to the basement inevitably excluded centaurs pleased Marcus to no small degree. Equally appealing, above the entrance, in large, smeared letters with the blackest paint, somehow defying the tunnel-like darkness of the stairway was the curt proclamation "NO TROLLS." The basement was, of course, dark, improbably larger than the bar above, spreading beneath the buildings along the entire block, the exposed brick of its deep grottos lit only occasionally by bare hanging bulbs humming the dimmest cerulean glow. The stairwell ended before a small bar. The rest of the basement's dingy antechamber was filled with worn stools pushed up against the wall. Two open doorways on opposite ends of the room led to a maze of corners and dark rooms. Marcus again let his eyes adjust to the dim light before approaching the bar to order a drink.

The bartender was a thin, vampire-like man in an ashen tuxedo shirt and limpid bow-tie, so pale Marcus wondered if he might not live down here, eking out a meager existence lapping up the various body fluids splashed upon the rank floors and walls of the sundry backrooms. His order of ambrosia, straight, no ice, was met with stoic compliance. As the ghoul poured his drink from a dusty bottle, Marcus, trying not to contemplate the cleanliness of the glass, surveyed the few souls hanging about.

A man emerged from the blackness of the nearest doorway. He stood there as if he had stepped from one country into another, unsure even of what language to speak. He spotted Marcus, and grounded by an unreturned recognition, gathered his wits to approach.

The man joined him at the bar and said simply, "Marcus."

Marcus blinked and said, "Hello," trying to place the face in the dim light.

The man had a soft, boyish complexion, very pale though, as if he had spent years in this very basement. Marcus was much annoyed that he, too, wore a baseball cap and leather jacket.

"You look so different from your days as a faun." The man spoke with an irritatingly dramatic flair. "My, my, I can't imagine you prancing around like that now."

Wearily, they looked each other up and down. Bruce, his name was Bruce, Marcus remembered. They used to skip through the brush of the Ramble together, meeting at Stables the next night to compare bite marks while centaurs bought them drinks. "Gods, did I let centaurs buy me drinks?" Marcus thought, overwhelmed by the rush of memories once so well-concealed.

Bruce, noticing his astonishment, feigned surprise. "Come on, it wasn't that long ago, Marcus. Surely you think of the good old days now and then."

Rather than reply, Marcus took a long drink. The ambrosia here was unfiltered, raw fuel for midnight jets. And he didn't come for the conversation. Bruce looked so different and yet the same. His wide-eyed confidence replaced by a calm expression, nothing approaching wisdom, more an urban practicality. He looked taller in jeans. He used to look so fresh and daring, naked with furry legs crossed gaily at the bar. Marcus wondered if he looked just as different to Bruce.

"I'm surprised to see you here anyway ... I had always thought you'd have turned werewolf by now."

Marcus finished his drink and smiled, showing all of his teeth, thinking with newfound clarity, "So did I. So did I."

Bruce knew from experience that really, there was no room for small talk at Pluto's. Having already sampled enough of the boys for the night, he went upstairs. Marcus redoubled his determination to forget everything, to lose himself in the labyrinth, to swim far enough from shore that land vanishes, all direction, the past, the future, the insufferable present, everything was rendered meaningless.

He crossed the room and entered the doorway opposite the dark portal from which Bruce had come. Again, his vision adjusted to a new level of darkness. Another antechamber. A lone blue bulb illuminated the sharp cameos of fauns restless against the far wall; Marcus gave them hard stares, challenging them to come and serve. He turned, parting the damp rubber curtain leading to the next room. The air was thick with cigarette smoke and the moans and gasps of men fondling men, penetrating one another in total abandon, fauns giving themselves over to whichever man first parted their buttocks, men who, when finished, would invite the next to partake of the

same hot, greasy flanks. Men and boys everywhere in the darkness exhaling the sweet satisfaction of savage intimacy with strangers; the beautiful knowledge that together they were an undulating canvas of flesh, groping, tearing, only to rejoin, painting one another with harsh indifference.

From behind, he felt a warm rush of flesh – reaching back with both hands, he grasped the thigh-hair of the two fauns that had followed him. Quickly, he turned and kissed one while placing his hand firmly on the other's shoulder, pushing him down toward his crotch. Both fauns readily complied. Two pretty boys greedily fed from his mouth and freed cock. Peeling down his jeans, the kneeling faun took the member thickening before him reverently in his hands. Kissing this power, he bent further, turning to place himself in total servitude beneath the lofty hang of testicles, corpulent gears to run his mouth. Marcus grasped the other faun's long, thin cock in one hand, running his thumb over the tightening foreskin, rhythmically milking him. With his other hand he guided the faun at his crotch to consume more of his heaving sack, grabbing him by the back of the neck to position a more immediate surrender. Cock now fully engorged, he reached around and dug at the tight hole of the faun he was still kissing. Probing for entry, he worked his fingers to part the tense warmth, making way for his hungry cock.

So bookended between two obedient boys, Marcus paused long enough to struggle out of his pants and jacket. Naked, he turned his backside to the kneeling faun as he forced the other to bend before him. As he plunged his dick, slick from a white lather of pre-cum, into the tender faun, the other boy furtively licked his ass, parting the swirl of his hair with a lissome tongue. Marcus primed his cock to thread the faun's inviting slit. The little creature, hands on his knees, bleated with pleasure.

While plundering one faun, he sensed a disturbance in the attention due his now saliva-soaked buttocks. Turning, he noticed another man had crept up in the darkness to roughly mount the faun behind him. Anger rose up in him, but his cock was far too involved in the animal crevice before him to allow for any altercation. Besides, he reminded himself, "Such is the nature of Pluto's Basement – there are no barriers of the flesh here."

With renewed concentration, he focused solely on the boy before him; the soft white violin of his torso bobbing in the darkness, afloat on a soundless sea. Marcus stretched out his hands to smooth the instrument of his pleasure. He felt a tongue dart into his ass again. A giddy equilibrium restored, Marcus pulled his burgeoning cock from out the faun and strung his

back with looping jets of cum – the poor young thing strained his neck and jaw, vainly lapping the air for a stray hot pearl.

He eased out from between the two fauns as other men rushed to fill the steamy vacuum. Everywhere, men hoisted fauns onto their laps, plugging their cocks into bleating boys. Men groped other men. Fauns sighed, men moaned. In one corner, a naked old man clutched the wall in a novel pose. He was remarkably skinny, his bald pate lively with sweat; he wore only a loose leather collar with metal spikes, his pale, withered rear was getting drilled, albeit awkwardly and without much finesse, by a faun earnestly bucking away, the pink triangle of his tongue comically stroking his upper lip in an act of stoic concentration.

The room was thick with the combined heat rising from men and boys, the scent of their sweat and cum electrical, ripe ingredients for a pending storm. And, already Marcus found himself getting hard again. He walked from room to room, observing the hot couplings, breathing in the rich animal odor.

In one room, two fauns relaxed against the wall kissing, backs arched, their bare, taunt bellies shone white and sinewy in the weak light. They gently stroked one another's small, rigid cocks, each with a matching halo of curly blonde hair, thighs lush with fur gold across lithe, goatish legs; Marcus was drawn

to them. Closer, he could just discern dullish spikes parting their curls. Both fauns possessed a set of small ivory horns. Each had similar sharp, upturned noses and smart, dark eyes that flashed like black tile hovering just beneath the surface of a cool, rejuvenating fountain. He stood before them, stroking his now fully erect cock, awaiting an invitation. Sensing his presence, the boys parted, looking at Marcus with approval. He stepped up and kissed one, then the other, the rich spice of their moist lips heightening his arousal. He cupped their supple asses, fingering the down of their ready cheeks. The fauns sighed in unison, their jutting cocks knocking against his muscular thighs, each with a boyish hand on his dick; they could barely wrap their fingers around its pulsing girth. He pulled them closer, kissing both, his grip on their buttocks equally firm. Their young fists slid from his cock as they unlocked their mouths from his and slowly lowered themselves in mutual worship.

Marcus placed his hands against the wall and groaned in pleasure as one faun sniffed at his testicles while the other gingerly stretched his lips around his wide head. He fingered their horns as they worked his cock and balls. His penis flush with mounting orgasm, he wished to fill the one faun's throat with his salt. Eyes closed, the boy was mesmerized by the metronomic force of the cock between his lips. The other kneeling faun catered to his balls, plump in the carriage of his

mouth. Marcus slipped his cock out of the faun's mouth to lift the trembling boy, turning him over on his knees – ass in the air, lubricated with sweat, a humming portal of ecstasy. Marcus played the head of his cock across the faun's quivering hole. The other faun lay on his back, working his dick slowly with one hand while lightly massaging the horns on his head with two fingers.

Marcus could no longer restrain himself. Breaking the boy's flanks, pushing his fury deep into the whimpering faun, finding a tight, resistant heat, he steered the faun's shoulder blades, increasing his speed to a punishing rhythm as the faun begged for mercy. His attractive twin rose to comfort the faun, stroking his cheeks and whispering assurances while eyeing Marcus, admiring his strong and towering form riding atop the suppliant youth. Marcus felt his second orgasm of the night build, and bracing himself, pushed his cock further and further into the faun, the boy's buttocks spread raw and wide, the drumming of pelvis to ass echoing within their personal grotto. He unleashed a roar of hot semen, the little faun groveled as Marcus pulled out, molten diamonds rolled across his back, spiking his neck.

Breathless, he collapsed atop the spent little faun, whose vigilant twin still caressed the boy's cheeks, cooing calming

noises, plaintive, yet his eyes roamed past Marcus, searching for the next figure to emerge from the darkness to deliver an ever-ephemeral fulfillment.

Marcus glanced at this horned silhouette; the very figure of his ever-looming desire momentarily appeared more the leering marionette than innocent prey. The black strings of their damp shadows were pulled taunt, through a barely perceivable crack in the floor. A red light from yet another basement world radiated from this fissure, hinting at other levels, those various avenues of desire so buried as to have surreptitious entrances and virtually no exit.

Chapter 6. The Centaur and the Faun

Everything comes gradually and at its appointed hour.

– Ovid

Bill stood by the bar in his usual spot, fingering his beard, trying not to lust after the surrounding young fauns, impatiently awaiting the barkeep to bring him a fresh cider; he'd sworn off ambrosia, at least for tonight. He had fretted through happy hour trying to come up with some alternative to drinking another weekend away, but after several frustrating hours trying to read a tedious novel that he had restarted several times until, finally exasperated, Bill sped out in a fury of thirst and boredom, barely able to notice traffic lights or tourists weary of being trampled. Another point of annoyance: it's not like he could even go somewhere else if he wanted to. Stables

was the only Faery bar in trotting distance, centaurs being barred from the subway. Obviously cabs were out of the question. Not to mention any building with stairs. Worse, for years he had endured paradisiacal tales of those fortunate souls lucky enough to turn centaur while summering on Fire Island, stranded by circumstance, blessed to forever frolic on white beaches, plucking fruit from trees, running down fauns in the dunes every spring. Though you would think the winters terrible, they hibernate in cozy barns stocked with cider and oats. The open beaches and wild surf invite long runs, so the centaurs there were slim and roasted a radiant bronze by the sun. Fauns of such an inclination trek there by the boatload all summer long, making for an enclave to envy from Bill's vantage point. Secretly, he imagined these tales grossly exaggerated, nobody mentioning the flea-to-centaur ratio on Fire Island, for instance (he had to use a rather expensive soap himself, not a common import among idyllic isles, or so he hoped).

Smiling to himself as the bartender finally brought him another cider, Bill thought his island offered much less in terms of tranquility but so much more in terms of available faundom. Here, Bill mostly stuck to Stables and, rarely, some of the other Greenwich Village bars. Though quick to catch up on his

nightly drinking, he was not so dedicated to imbibing cider to overlook the fine young herd currently parading about the bar.

Several shy-looking fauns had already slinked out into the night. Probably building up the courage to make their first forays into the Ramble, Bill thought. And there goes that handsome man; he looked like he was waiting for something to happen. Maybe he had a date with that cute faun from last night. Though maybe not. Men and fauns rarely engage in anything that lasts more than one night these days. And so Bill sighed, thinking how that particular man always seemed so calm and content, and reminisced about his own nights chasing faun, allowing his recollections to stretch the compass of his past embraces, lacing them with sweeter emotions that may or may not have been as present or as pronounced then as in memory; the song of memory always lasts longer than the dance. Such sentimentality meant he was well on his way to getting happily drunk. Just then he noticed a small, lithe faun sheepishly smiling at him.

Bill retained just enough composure not to look over his shoulder and see who the faun's smile was really meant for; his mind raced down the terrible, scorched path of past lessons learned. "What does he want?" "Is he a prostitute?" "I don't have any money." "Is he one of those fauns who just like to

torment old centaurs, buttering them up with flattery only to skip off into the night?"

Luckily he veered right off of this road and landed in the woods of his own natural instinct – he merely returned the faun's smile with a casual wave of his hand and patted the barstool beside him. The faun bound across the room and leapt up on the stool, quickly tucking his meek penis between crossed legs. With nervous fingers the faun combed the long, shiny reddish-blonde pelt flourishing across his thighs, consuming his ankles, sweeping to a ragged fringe over scuffed, dirty hooves.

The boy timidly but formally stuttered out an introduction. Bill shook the faun's extended hand, smiling in admiration of the rare civility. Since he was completely naked, Bill thought the boy must be new to the city. Urban fauns always go out in a fresh shirt high on their midriff or at least some version of the latest fashion – a thin, loose belt hanging off their skinny waist, somehow always accentuating the bald little pricks kneeling in prayer just below. Bill asked how long he had been in the city, and took a long pull of his cider to control his thumping heart; he hoped to somehow staunch the initial quivering of his moistening cock.

The boy beamed up at him, his wide, dark eyes wet with nervous excitement, the absurd, rhythmic cuckoo-cuckoo clock of his Adam's apple working overtime to submerge his juvenile nervousness. Bill noticed the youthful freckles painted across the lad's cheeks and shoulders. Straightening himself up to his full impressive height, hoping his stomach did not look especially distended, Bill launched into the advice veteran city dwellers typically give to virgins. Virgins. His penis bounced between his legs at the thought. This boy is a virgin. It is an occasional practice among faun virgin to first partner with a centaur. Some find it instructive and ready practice while a few take to the encounter enough to make it their main desire. Too few. "This boy wants me to initiate him in preparation for the Ramble!" Bill could no longer contain himself – his penis swung out with such a force it slapped the floor, flinging sawdust into the startled boy's face. All Bill could do was stand proud and let his massive, scarlet cock hold sway between his splayed legs.

The faun, hypnotized, said those magic words uttered by every faun formally requesting initiation from a centaur. "Sir - sir, may I – I study under you?"

Bill's entire being shuddered in delight, his cock flogging the floor in consent.

Near midnight, Barrett stirred from the couch and went to the kitchen to peer once again into the luminous, cool maw of the cavernous refrigerator, hoping that with this visit he might somehow discern something approaching edible among the pittance of impotent condiments and soggy carrots. No such luck. Though broke, he was not in the mood to go to the bars and graze on pretzels, waiting for some drunken centaur to buy him drinks. That last evening in the Ramble was so enriching, he did not yet want to water down the memory with a fresh experience; his buttocks tingled with the recollection.

Earlier, he and Hector had had enough foresight to stretch their previous conversation, allowing Christopher to slip out of the apartment seemingly undetected, navigating his own nocturnal destiny (tradition among the Faery Folk of New Amsterdam dictates that faun make their first foray into the Ramble alone). So Hector gossiped with Barrett; both fauns determining that the soon-to-be-due rent, coupled with their ever hungry tails twitching for attention, necessitated their participation in the next Banquet. Soon afterward, Hector left to scour the bars for an invite from fauns in the know. And thus Barrett endured the rare night home, home being their fifth floor walk-up on the outskirts of Chelsea. Not too far from the popular bars, though the long shadows of the projects hovered near, with ruined piers just south of the nearby highway,

elements that had long made their neighborhood an affordable haven to young Faeries.

Sprawled on the couch, Barrett leafed through old magazines, the television on low. He thought about what was happening to Hector, how it would happen to him at some future point in time. The change. Lately everything Hector did was colored with a newfound resolve. At the Ramble, he was the first to raid the foliage, the last to leave. The sun was nearly fully crowned, the streets thick with commuters rushing to work when Hector would emerge, shaking the cool waters of Bethesda fountain from his freshly dipped rear to the surprise of secretaries and accountants raising suitcases and purses alike to deflect the droplets flying from his shiny coat. A faun's coat only has that glimmer when he's a young foal or when he is about to shed his faundom and enter manhood. Hector's shoulders looked broader, manly. He did not skip through the park so much as move with a determined maturity. Of the fauns that Barrett knew, he was the oldest. Soon he would turn, shedding his enchantment to become … human.

And, men stay men. Men recall their faundom as if a dream, a humid dream, a long, droll movie dream seen at some now-closed drive-in on a cloudy summer night. Such gray men are usually the most dismissive toward the Faery Folk, making

rude comments to their anxious wives while passing them on the street, demanding police ticket any centaur urinating in public (when actually it is only against the law on Sundays).

Some men remember; they are drawn back into the park as if their Faery youth had turned narcotic, the smoke of memory hooking them by the nose, pulling them back to the playground of their previous mischief. This is not mortal mischief, however. These shadows bite. And then there are the shadows found in the bottom of a glass. Some men who remember would like to forget. And for some drowning their thoughts in ambrosia and neglect excites a bit of the Faery spark that resides in everyone, excites it to a monstrous degree that such men metamorphose into centaurs, lumbering through Washington Square, fouling the Arch, snatching at any passing faun, those living candle flames that dance away from their gross clutches, as nimble and intangible as the memories they failed to dissolve.

Well, at least I'll never become a centaur, I get sleepy after just two glasses of ambrosia, Barrett thought as he shifted on the couch. He wondered if he would likely turn werewolf, though becoming a man seemed equally unimaginable, much less the consequences, for he was still of an age where any metamorphosis seemed as singular as an eclipse, not inevitable

as a season. More privately, far from the surface of his consciousness, he entertained the thought no faun ever verbalizes. "What if I don't change?" And they do exist. The Immortals. Those forever faun, the most celebrated of Faery Folk, whose very existence positively demonstrates that their nearly diluted divinity sprang long ago from somewhere eternal. Their names, once the impetus for ancient rhyme, now splash across tabloid headlines. *Zodiac Today* in particular is dedicated to following their exploits, providing exposés on the endless parties or worse, sordid photographs of once famous fauns caught buying flea powder at K-Mart; promised in next month's issue, the first glimpse of a nymph whose beauty felled empires, long in seclusion, now behind on her rent, living above a gas station in Fort Lauderdale. Still, most maintain a celebrity above reproach, retired Gods in the aforementioned sunglasses. All their names legend, though none shine like Ganymede, most recently infamous (within the confines of the present century, that is) for his Oscar speech decades ago where, thanking the Academy for their appreciation of his role in the silent film version of *A Midsummer Night's Dream*, he spoke in Greek, not yet having learned English, claiming afterwards to an adoring press the language nothing more than a passing fad. And of course, this further elevated his stature in France.

Barrett turned the pages of a well-thumbed copy of *Zodiac*. But they are very few in number. Jet-setting in Concords, Crete to New Amsterdam weekends to flirt with the werewolves of Central Park, old Europe having long been depleted of the luxury of their dangerous embrace. Barrett tried to imagine such a life for himself. Immortality was as equally unimaginable as mortality. Maybe I would be handsome as a man. I don't want to be a werewolf. However, I will miss the chase. And Barrett thought of Hector again, that his next exit from the Ramble would possibly be his last as a faun. And young Christopher, it was after midnight, and he had not come home. Barrett closed the magazine. Pulling at the knots in the unruly hair of his thighs, seemingly impossible to untangle, he curled his hooves under his rump and yawned. It was one of those youthful yawns, that stretching of every muscle that gives you, in an instant, a measure of your entire being, a sturdy hinge for the entire universe.

Asterion. Southern boys have such mythic names. And really, the more impoverished the boy, the more grandiloquent the name. Of course Bill kept his thoughts to himself as he galloped down Seventh Avenue. He struggled to maintain a casual pace while keeping the conversation light. Commenting on passing sights of historical importance, the boy lopping beside him, Bill pointed out the fenced grounds of the old

women's prison, now a library, where witches and warlocks were burned at the stake during the witch-hunts of the mid-fifties. Asterion nodded solemnly as Bill shuddered to think that a horror so common to his childhood was already ancient lore to one so young.

Taxis roared past the couple, intimidating the boy. Bill put his hand on his shoulder and guided him down one of the quieter, tree-shrouded streets. Not the quickest route but seductively serene; after all, real estate is a large part of New Amsterdam's allure. Bill felt so good having his hand on the shoulder of such a wonderful boy that, he thought if the night ended here, he could go home content. Seeing Asterion's graceful figure cowed by the city, by all of the thoughts and fears he must harbor about the experience he was about to embark on, Bill immediately sobered. He realized his duty to a fellow member of the Faery Folk. Catching the boy's eye, he gave him a reassuring smile, squeezing his shoulder. The faun looked up at him gratefully, sure in his choice of tutors. They arrived at his building. Bill gently ushered him in.

Turning on the lights, Bill thought, what a mess. But better yet, he liked that the apartment resembled who he was. This is the real me. Sure, there were overturned books and dishes in the sink, but the music stand stood proud, a rickety

pulpit for his more introverted endeavors; these were the things that made it home. He shot the boy a quick look. The faun took a deep breath, and Bill instinctively knew the boy felt comfortable, welcomed.

After lighting some candles, Bill turned out the lights. He leaned down and gave the faun a gentle kiss. Asterion, flush in making the right choice, nearly collapsed into Bill's arms, his inexperienced mouth open to the possibilities the centaur was eager to impose. Relieved, Bill at last let his long cock expand its true equine girth, finally proud rather than embarrassed, knowing a young faun was here to receive his splendor. And receive it he did. Parting his lips, Asterion knelt down before him, shaking with the righteous fear of the initiate. Bill stroked his head and smiled, knowing his horse-cock was much too daunting for the willing mouth. And the faun was as perplexed as he was nervous and aroused, trying to wrestle the slippery, impertinent cock in his small hands, bringing the thick crimson phallus close to his eager lips but not really knowing what to do. Bill willfully demanded restraint from his throbbing cock, calming the faun equally with another gentle kiss, finally laying on his side, face to face with the boy, his wide, red pole now less intimidating, more accessible. The faun relaxed into Bill's large, equestrian form, melding into the heated space between the centaur's bent legs and engorged member.

A faun in worship, kissing and stroking Bill's horse-cock, kneading a certain ecstasy from the centaur; globular pearls of pre-cum crowned his penis. Bill neighed with delight as the boy rose to nimbly mount his pole, wrapping one hoof around it as if ready to launch himself heavenward. Mutual ecstasy, mutual sighs: the cry of the initiate finally given over to his totem, the centaur's drought at an end, one hoof knocking the floor in immutable elation. Bill reached up to strum his fingers across the boy's ever available ass, Asterion immediately sighing in rapture, lowered his quivering bottom to beg attention, granting Bill deeper access to his pink crescent. As he eased a deliberate finger into the boy, the faun continued to feast on the length of cock before him, nibbling, licking, kissing the head, teething on the meaty lips, the pink pout of Bill's slit, a steady stream of warm semen bubbling forth.

Bill craved the impossible. He wanted in. Asterion sensed this, ceasing his oral administrations to look at Bill. As they looked into one another's eyes, a candle sputtered out. Their gaze deepened with the enveloping darkness; Asterion solemnly gave silent assent. Bill rolled over on his back as the boy positioned himself precariously before his rigid horse-cock. Even getting the head in would be nearly impossible, but the youth seemed determined, possessed by the ruby serpent pulsing between his legs. Bill felt the soft, tight buttocks

73

nestling against his cockhead, the tight hole unwinding to permit his desire. He could no longer withhold orgasm; grasping the boy by the wrists to steady himself, his semen flooded out in hot rivulets, coursing over the boy's proffered buttocks, thick waves of horse-cream waxing his shoulders. Several hot darts of fluid spiraled into the boy's receptive sphincter – he bucked as if lightning struck his spine. His own climax rising, he launched a slim gooey white dove toward the ceiling, arching high above Bill's sweaty brow.

When the youth collapsed backward to lie across Bill's supine form, he was panting heavily, encased in the cooling, sticky amber of their golden delight. Feeling more satiated than he had in years, Bill marveled at the damp head of hair nestling on his chest. While absently stroking the faun, he thought of gently repositioning him so he could grab some towels, but as he entertained this thought, his breathing, too, slowed, eyes closing for a moment's respite. Quite quickly, he joined Asterion in a deep, unhurried sleep, unhurried because what was left unfinished between them was not cause for regret but continuance. Asterion let loose a flurried snore. Instinctively, Bill shifted his bulk to better accommodate the boy.

Chapter 7. The Werewolves of Wall Street

Remember that in life you ought to behave as at a banquet.

– Epictetus

Barrett examined his reflection, made angelic in the cloudy mirror. Vapors of steam from his recent shower anointed the glass. A devilish grin broke the illusion. Christopher had burst into the tiny bathroom to share his cologne, flashing broad, handsome white teeth in the rapidly clearing surface. Their two faces looked beautiful together. And tonight they would share a singular feast. To better excite and please their hosts, they pulled on matching black sleeveless T-shirts with loose, tattered necklines, cut high over their taut abdomens.

The thought of another Banquet infused Barrett with nervous anticipation, though this was Christopher's first. Where Barrett was exhilarated, he was subdued, having heard tales of such violent eroticism that, of all the new experiences he was currently awash in, this one could prove either most enriching … or treacherous.

Barrett gave him a brotherly kiss and ushered him toward the door. They bound down the groaning stairs, pushing past other fauns heading either to the park or the bars. Heads held high, noses in the air, they rushed past with all due hauteur. Their journey tonight was a step beyond the Ramble, into a rarefied darkness less defined, thus it was necessarily to steel themselves from the other fauns.

The Ramble had borders, for sure, but the Banquet required invitations.

The boys splurged on a cab and held hands on the way uptown, having huddled conspiratorially behind a battered mailbox while a coerced human waved down a taxi for them. This evening's Banquet was to be held at the penthouse of a prominent werewolf, on the top floor of one of New Amsterdam's more renowned skyscrapers. The doorman waved

them toward a private elevator of polished brass that dispatched them skyward.

Christopher smiled weakly and whispered, "It feels like we're going to the moon."

The moon was full, every werewolf at the apex of his lust. Christopher let go of Barrett's hand as the elevator came to a stop and its doors parted.

The penthouse did possess something of a lunar atmosphere. The elevator opened into a spacious living room; large, pale ferns curled in upon themselves on either side of the entrance, alien fauna demarcating a world unique itself. A long window revealed the cut of the city, a panorama so bright it banished the stars, the only visible celestial body the low lying moon, burnishing Central Park with a dusty silver hue. The apartment was minimally furnished; this was a lair, not a home, filled with manicured men relaxing in stark kimonos, observing the arrival of the fauns with a cool detachment, as if they were reviewing a well-thumbed menu at a much-frequented restaurant.

Christopher stood awestruck until Hector ushered them into the room. He looked more and more a man everyday, Barrett thought, as Hector displayed them to a pair of quiet,

still-human werewolves, a reassuring hand on Christopher's shoulder. Hector had recently sprouted some slight hair on his chin. His chest had broadened and his nipples, too, were encircled with fresh, blondish curls. The pelt of his thighs had thinned to the point where, excepting his shiny hooves, he looked more a statuesque marathon runner than a member of the Faery Folk. Barrett noticed that his penis, too, had taken on more manly proportions.

Playfully, he reached for it and teasingly asked, "Are you trying to give the wolves a run for their money, Hector?"

Blushing, Hector swatted his hand away and gave them both a stern look, silently reminding them that they were not just among werewolves but here strictly for their pleasure. Here the playfulness of the park was inappropriate, possibly dangerous. Barrett straightened himself up and dropped his smile, but not without noticing that Hector's penis had thickened, ever so slightly, from the attention.

They strolled into the dining room where several men stood, absently fingering their robust chests through loosened robes, examining the passing fauns with the nonchalance of seasoned auction-goers. There were other fauns as well, though they were outnumbered by men. This imbalance was an integral

part of the Banquet; an uneven match ensures that the hunters must vie for the prey.

Within the youthful gathering, Barrett noticed Destri, who was easily among the most beautiful boys of the fauns who frequented Stables and, occasionally, the Ramble. Tall for a faun, Destri struck a rather brash contrapposto pose, naked except for a stunning gold chain necklace, likely a gift bestowed from a previous Banquet. Originally from Spain, where fauns are a rarity and tend to be short and dark, as clannish as Syrian satyrs and equally disinclined to immigrate, he was thus considered quite a delicacy among the werewolves. His complexion was tan, however, with a golden tint likely earned on Fire Island, and it was highlighted by the flaxen, luxuriant down that covered his thighs and shaggy buttocks. His pert cock was erect, its tiny dark head peeking out from beneath a silky sheath of foreskin as he conversed in close whispers with two men, both obviously enamored with him. Hector and Christopher adopted the more docile poses of the fauns about the room, hoping a suitable werewolf would choose them as dining companions, thus sparing them the orgiastic quarrels that normally follow dinner.

As yet, none of the men had begun their transformation. This, too, was a formality, though there is no lessening in the

sharpness of tooth after such constrained bestiality. Such reeled passion, when finally unleashed, becomes more torrential than what could be expected of the typical carnivore. Again, the Wolves of Wall Street are a breed apart from the beasts that prowl Central Park. These were wolves of such power that they easily broke the spell of the Ramble, casting their own lupine enchantment wherever they chose to meet. As with their wealth, so, too, is their lycanthropy more pronounced. When the men here shift, they take to the wolf form more fully, leaving their humanity farther behind, cast off in tatters on the carpet. The older wolves, of which there were many, possess lush silver and white coats. They wantonly shake loose their humanity as if shuffling off a bothersome constraint until nothing is left – rough paws on the floor, elongated teeth ever-ready to sharpen anew on the backs of many, many boys. Even in human form, lupine characteristics are subtly apparent. These are men who will never drop a fork at dinner and always appear at ease. Full, deep, nearly carnivorous eye contact is one of their trademarks. The hunt pervades every aspect of their lives. And that just may be the primary difference, what sets them apart from the nocturnal kingdom of the Ramble; they are not governed by the moon, by lust. They govern themselves – werewolves in sleek suits, at midnight in Battery Park, converging on their prey, a lone faun who missed the last ferry to his Staten Island haven.

Wolves growling low, in unison with the surf lapping angrily at the seawall. Or, limousine werewolves shred leather seats circling Pluto's Basement in long, shiny cars, waiting for exiting fauns to hop among the traffic, innocently hoping for a ride. Or, werewolves climbing skyscrapers, naked save silk, wind-flogged ties, the cars below a stream of wispy neon insects. So howl the Werewolves of Wall Street.

A handsome, dark-complexioned man in a loosely-wrapped kimono of black silk introduced himself to Barrett. Barrett tried not to show how intimidating he found the still-human werewolf's height, his dark ebony skin, magnificently broad shoulders, a striking baldness, his high, arched brow shone like bronze. A quick bolt of panic that this, indeed might be the werewolf Bane receded within him as quickly as it had struck. Bane, legend or not, could obviously never be bound by such restricted, mannered proceedings. Still, Barrett was disturbed to have been so suddenly separated from Christopher. As this was his first Banquet, Barrett had hoped to pair the youngster with a wolf of some distinction before he allowed himself to be partnered. The Dark Wolf read Barrett's confusion as fear and his attraction deepened. Barrett could not help but be struck by the mature beauty of the werewolf towering before him; his black and emerald eyes held the depths and shadows of a forgotten forest, flecks of yellow among the sinister green

hinted at sunlight filtered through a myriad of thick leaves. Full lips parted in a smile of utter confidence. His kimono was pulled taunt across stomach muscles bunched like boulders gathering to announce the avalanche of a thick, round cock barely holstered beneath the tie of his sash. Ready to explore this lethal topography, Barrett felt compelled to lower himself before this man-wolf right then and there, to offer himself as his total slave and living tool. His jaw slackened. Eyes closed, he shuddered at the impending surrender, knowing it was too soon; the formality of the Banquet dictated another course of action.

He gathered his strength and nodded deferentially to his newfound master. Barrett had hoped to at least be seated near Christopher and wondered if any of the werewolves he'd been introduced to at the last Banquet would be present, that way he could steer the young faun toward one whose appetite precluded blood.

Dinner was served.

Everyone was silently ushered into the dining room by the evening's only attendant, a weird Faery of an indeterminable genus, pale and thin in an overly-starched tuxedo, its face waxen and withered though alert, as if an unwrapped mummy had been taken by surprise. The wide discs

of his pupil-less eyes held the dim phosphorescence of wanton servitude; whatever the creature had once been had seceded willingly, ages ago, into this slavish state, one of many lives used and forgotten in the world of wolves.

They were seated at a long table of silvery dishes filled with rocky peppers toppling over caramelized onions above which guttering candles tossed a low, sinister cathedral of light. Bowls of small, glossy apples glowed so dark as to appear chocolate, and were intermittently laced with black sprigs of mint. Raw oysters were served on tiny, nearly translucent china dishes the shape of seashells that flickered blue when raised before a candle. All was interspersed with bunches of fruit. Petulant grapes rolled loose about the table, potent with the promise of fermentation. The werewolves and their guests were poured blood red wine from thick, open-mouthed crystal carafes. Light fare all, edible trinkets, known aphrodisiacs or dishes requested by senior wolves. Satisfaction would come later, though not before everyone was served a small, delicate shimmer of Phoenix custard. Rumored the very taste of immortality, the table in its entirety was obviously impressed by this rarest of delicacies, though secretly Barrett thought it tasted more like a buttery salmon. The dinner also consisted of erotic murmurings among those werewolves who had already chosen their fauns.

Those wolves yet to deign which faun or fauns would serve them assessed the prospects from around the table, genially discussing business, mostly things Barrett did not understand, mergers and acquisitions. Apparently for the werewolves assembled here no aspect of life lay outside the hunt.

As dinner concluded, silence reigned. Barrett, with one hand on the strong, supple thigh of the Dark Wolf, knew he had been chosen for the night and thus was safe. At the other end of the table, several wolves were eying Christopher, all highly aroused. Hector, seated next to Destri, lost his partner to the silent bidding for Christopher. Forlornly, he looked on as Destri, slowly fingering his gold necklace, masterfully seduced the silver-haired werewolf eying him from across the table.

The evening was about to start in earnest.

Hosts and fauns rose. The fish-thing waiter quickly collected kimonos, laying them meticulously across his cadaverous coat rack arm. As the lights suddenly dimmed, Christopher let out a terrified gasp. Murmurs turned to dim growls. As they moved into the other room, the shift was upon the pack. Men shed their kimonos as their backs broadened, darkening with the gloss of an emerging coat. For those who

simply could not contain themselves, or who found the sound of ripping fabric a crucial part of the game, the purr of torn silk whispered throughout the room. And so exquisite kimonos, centuries old, sewn from thread blackened with dragon blood by the blind eunuchs of Imperial Chinese courts now dust, were shred by lupine chests bursting forth from their silken barriers, heaving with newly-formed strength and desire.

The Werewolves of Wall Street emerged Animal. Feral souls burst through weak, human husks.

In the Ramble, you never witness a transformation so much as sense it, a shift among the shadows, beast-sounds in the distance. Though Barrett had attended past Banquets, he was still in awe of the physical spectacle before him. Wolves howled, eyes shut as new muscle molded their skeletons, fur strained through pores, teeth lengthened, black tears of exertion dampened new pelts. They howled with an animal glee.

Several wolves surrounded an effusively panting Christopher. He was filled with terror, struck dumb from witnessing the startling, mass metamorphosis. Barrett could not come to his aid. The Dark Wolf had completed his shift and swayed carnivorously before him. Trembling, Barrett knelt. His monster-suitor stood arms out, grinning down as his tremendous totem rose haughtily before the suppliant faun. Barrett, choked

with desire, leaned in to inspect this pulsing animal passion, rubbing his cheek against the massive dark flat head, licking the glutinous pre-cum that had begun to gather in the sneer of the cock's gristly spout, the wolf's penis so huge he could hoist the thing in both hands like a hefty, iron goblet. As the faun tongued his salty slit, the werewolf howled in delight. Barrett continued to suckle at the beast as his tender hole began to moisten in a sweaty plea for attention. The werewolf sensed this and plunged one long, sharp claw far into Barrett's quivering buttocks. With his other claw, he cajoled Barrett to open his mouth wide to accommodate his ravenous member. Barrett had to straighten his neck and torso to properly meet the commanding cock. Tears of joy and pain streamed down his cheeks as he embarked upon an impossible consumption; the Dark Wolf knowingly played his claws lightly against the dual harp of his buttocks, caressing the sweat-dampened down swirling around the faun's pink entry. The wolf's cock hung with a girth so massive it felt almost like a separate animal trying to burrow into him. And Barrett surrendered. His throat now occupied territory, his ass begged for invasion. The madness sparking throughout the room was a light cacophony compared to the orchestral rhythm that filled his mouth.

All about, werewolves cornered fauns or brought them down roughly to the floor. The large room was barren of any

furniture; the long windows providing the only light, the distant glow from sentinel skyscrapers illuminated the dark couplings. The faun Destri stood, legs spread wide, pulling his round, firm buttocks apart for his gray werewolf's inspection. The werewolf worked his muzzle into the boy like a key, supping at his backside, sharpening his fangs in the sacrificial slit. Turning to his werewolf compatriots, he let loose a glass-shattering howl of satisfaction, one that reverberated throughout the vast penthouse; an animal chord had been struck. The orgy commenced.

Across the room, three werewolves encircled Christopher, hairy cocks fully engorged. The boy, convulsing with fear and confusion, dropped to his knees. They growled and struck at one another as their stiff cocks sparred before the boy's face, probing the air for his young, wanton mouth. Christopher spun on his knees, unsure which wolf would claim him, how the spurned werewolves would react. Terrified of the consequences should they fight over him or attempt to share him, he cowered, lowering himself further to the floor. The werewolves were heaving in erotic exasperation, none wanting to share the boy, none willing to back down. The bulbous head of one cock found its way into Christopher's grateful mouth. With relief, he fell upon the cock, gulping at the immense presence jamming his throat, using his hands to squeeze and

caress the two other ample cocks, hoping to appease every wolf and stave off any brutal rape that might result from their joint fury.

In the room's center, the silver wolf devoured Destri's ass while Hector knelt before the Spanish faun, gingerly licking his cock. The gray wolf finally decided he had deposited enough saliva into the faun to guarantee the vigorous access he required. As the werewolf rose, Hector assisted him by standing and pushing Destri's head down to his own ready member. This older wolf, with coarse, bristly silver hair peppered black, barred his chipped ivory teeth at Hector while plunging his thick red rod deep into Destri's eager wet opening. The force of entry pushed the Spanish faun's mouth to the root of Hector's thickening cock. All three basked in the electrical ecstasy that their trinity generated.

The ebony wolf mastering Barrett's mouth pulled his cock out and with sure claws forced the faun down on all fours; Barrett readied himself for the shock of impact – still surprised, always surprised, the bolt of pain unwrapping within him, submerging all other sensations, such was this great demand. And the werewolf had worked just the blunt tip of his cock into the shallow of his buttocks. The boy bit his lip against the pain, fearing a loss of consciousness, relishing the knowledge that the

mammoth cock slowly cleaving his sanity would push him past the edge of a most delicious darkness.

With masterful patience, the werewolf paused to let his full length grow. And then he probed deeper. Barrett's entire body shook. The boy felt a certain fire consume the pain as every thrust lit the fabric of his soul. For one delirious moment, Barrett sincerely believed that if he opened his mouth in protest sparks would tumble out. What he dared not utter issued uncontrollably from his cock; weak little white flags of cum fluttered across the floor, one fleck hitting his chin, there to dangle, a delicate metronome to the motion of the werewolf navigating his backside.

Hector, hand atop Destri's sweaty brow, enjoyed the full lips scrubbing his scrotum. The werewolf delivered such a furious momentum the battered faun was propelled forward to swallow Hector in his entirety, nose bent against the other faun's abdomen, tears darkening the slight wisps of pubic hair that had so recently begun to encircle Hector's cock. The gray wolf broke his concentration upon the buttocks split before him to look Hector in the eye. Fear gripped Hector's soul as the werewolf's steely, feral gaze gave him a penetrating, silent command. Hector obeyed, sending a huge flood of semen into Destri's wet open mouth while the wolf, too, with a sonorous

howl, buried himself to the hilt of the boy's battered rear. His torso hummed between them, a mere conduit, the bolting threads of their semen linking together within the faun, this winding helix twisting tightly, erupting from his own cock a furious gold.

Christopher was the center of an ever-tightening knot of dark muscle. Hunched wolves clashed above him, their animal heat blinding, nearly suffocating the faun. Tough fur scoured his face and shoulders raw, his entry a well dug by animal fists. So many claws serrated him, his seat was moist with blood and animal sweat. Eventually, braised by cock and limb, he swooned. And was up, up in the air, a living crucifix bright but broken, greedily mounted, wolf after wolf working his backside and mouth, his wilted form sloppy with their joint drool – likely the only thing that saved him from grievous injury as cock after cock slipped swiftly into his stretched and succulent hole, plying his cavity, mining him, determined to find their own treasures in his shaft. Wolf after wolf plundered the boy to the point of release, release after compounding release until their semen flowed back out of him as he lay bent on the floor. With every ragged breath, more and more of this coagulating milk issued forth from his depths, soothing the worn, ruddy petals of his up-ended rump. Wolf semen flecked his bruised lips, his blonde hair black with sweat and spittle. His form lay calm, an

island smoothed by the storm. Nearly comatose, he glowed with a budding fever. He was radiant. After all, a collapsed temple is a terrifyingly beautiful thing.

Simultaneously, Barrett and Hector searched the room for Christopher. Their werewolves had met their pleasure and abandoned them. Overturned candles ran strange shadows up the walls, irrigating the darkness with fountains of demented light, illuminating spent werewolves pulling on trousers. Other animals returned to the dining room in naked glory to further sup on unfinished dishes of fruit and leftover griffin. Some slept where they had fallen, on their backs, already dreaming of even more lucrative hunts, a lone leg absently twitching in the air. Others stood about in open kimonos, their lethal cocks swaggering between strong thighs. No wolf had resumed human form. For those fauns wishing to stay, dawn would reward them with further physical plunder and even more treasure. As it was, Barrett and Hector wished to collect what crumpled bills or gold baubles were now being distributed as quickly as possible and then take Christopher home, having found him, an upbraided dandelion unconscious on the floor, a living battlefield smeared pink with a tapioca of blood and semen.

Dessert had been served.

Chapter 8. Every Dream a Forest

As the same fire assumes different shapes when it consumes objects differing in shape, so does the one Self take the shape of every creature in whom he is present.

– Marcus Aurelius

Bill awoke late into the afternoon, satiated, the absence of a hangover as pleasantly welcome as any spring day. It took him a few lazy moments to realize he was alone. Recalling the night's revelry, he smiled, imagining the boy sneaking out early in the morning. Maybe I'll see him again at Stables. We'll say "Hello," of course. But I won't be too pushy. I know how these boys are, skipping from one trick to another. I'll just count myself lucky to have had the pleasure of his company for one night. In fact, if I see him I'll tell him that straight away, so he

won't be shy about talking to me again. Bill enjoyed the rush of embarrassing thoughts; he had long grown accustomed to the social realities of his fellow Faery Folk. Still, as he moved about his apartment, righting chairs and restacking books, he could not help but linger over the sweeter kisses of the night before. It was too soon, was it not, to file away such passion into the dusty, ever-receding catalogue of past nameless encounters? Asterion. Bill smiled at the name while he boiled some water for coffee. No, not a nameless encounter. One to be savored. And these days they're coming less and less frequently. He turned to his closet and examined his aging, pitiable collection of shirts, wondering which one he should wear tonight; in case he saw the faun again he wanted to look his best, like someone Asterion would be proud to introduce his young friends to. Possibly, he might go out this afternoon, trot up to Chelsea and shop for a new shirt. The hiss of water boiling over interrupted his daydreaming.

Embarrassed, having caught himself already pining for the boy, planning for unlikely scenarios, he took the battered pot over to the sink and poured himself a cup of coffee. He looked at the grimy sink and noticed he only had one chipped coffee cup. Years of habit, repetition, disappointments, all had honed his life to be a life lived alone.

Just as his thoughts turned to his burgeoning hunger, a weak knock came at his door. *Probably that old witch from upstairs, always wanting a strand of hair from my tail for some spell. Oh well, she makes a nice newt-cake during the holidays.* As Bill wearily pulled the door open, he was startled to see Asterion laboring mightily under a bountiful barrel of apples. Bill leapt to the faun's aid as the barrel gave way and lusty red fruit bounced across the floor. They laughed, chasing errant apples happily about the room. When the last apple was gathered, Bill leaned down to kiss Asterion while the boy settled comfortably on the bed to drink the rest of Bill's cooling coffee from his lone but ample cup.

Marcus walked back from the gym feeling annoyed. Usually a workout helped him relax, the burn simmering within his trapezium muscles a sure sign he had pushed himself enough. Even the steam room wasn't particularly relaxing, filled as it was with trolls, grunting trolls, always fumbling with their towels or dropping their clubs. Lately, the gym was thick with trolls. Already, a knot of muscle, why they sought gym membership was beyond Marcus. Of all the Faery Folk, where fauns are, well, fawned over and centaurs frowned upon, trolls were universally considered repellent by the populace at large, human and Faery alike. Conversely, they were the most

successful in finding their niche, though really such was the nature of trolls.

Early immigrants to the city, among the first of the enchanted to arrive, as bridges began to stretch from the outer boroughs toward New Amsterdam proper, trolls slinked into position. Their labor legendary, they stayed and settled. Their numbers multiplied as the city grew into a spidery mass of bridges and overpasses, trolls living beneath them, laying brick, setting the massive wires, slavishly collecting coins from within the confines of their troll booths. They certainly annoyed Marcus more than centaurs, likely because they could access more places, and dirt from their clubs always muddied up the locker rooms. Still, their bodies in the steam room, their knobby knees of green flesh looked like faraway hills, a place where he could finally … what? Lately his thoughts were a jumble. Nor was work really satisfying.

Usually, the controlled bustle of the department store made him feel like one of the calm stewards of the city. Formerly, the satisfaction he brought his customers was fulfilling to the extreme. Now his days seemed listless. At work, he felt trapped inside. After work, in the bars, he felt uneasy and distracted.

The afternoon was more humid than usual, so the walk home was another source of annoyance. When he arrived at his apartment, he suddenly recalled a possible source of his discomfort. He had not felt right since that cute little faun had stayed the night. No, not the faun. The dream he had that night crystallized in his mind. He recalled the images: a small forest rose from his floor, surrounding his bed. He sat up and marveled at the small world of hills and treetops beyond his bedposts. Wanting to inspect this phenomenon, he reached to turn on the lamp; as he pulled the cord, the very moon hovered by his hand. He leapt back from the scalding coldness of its light. And he was no longer in bed but on the ground, looking up at impossibly large, looming trees, dark against the night's sky, stars bent on the barely perceptible contours of the ceiling and walls, weirdly punctuated by his open bedroom window, revealing further dimensions of night. Distant werewolves bayed. Naked, he turned to run toward the safety of his now mountainous bed. Werewolves howled again, closer. In a panic, he crashed through the woods. Limbs and branches reached for him as he passed.

He came to a small outcropping of rock and paused, noticing a dark crevice, he secreted himself inside. Marcus turned within the darkness and felt the dimensions of the damp cave. Peering outside to see if the pursuing beasts had arrived,

he was not startled to find the entrance now barred by thick, iron rod. Instead of fear, he felt something else. Finally, he welcomed the grip of impending justice.

Barrett returned from the bathroom with a fresh washcloth to cool Christopher's forehead. The boy was in the twelfth hour of a deep sleep. They had brought him back to the apartment as soon as decorum allowed; thankfully, the Dark Wolf graciously gave them the use of his private car and driver, as no cab would stop for two fauns struggling with a third, unconscious youth. The magnificent gold cufflinks, he awarded Barrett sat on the dresser. The glow of the cufflinks far exceeded the luster typical of fine metallurgy. They dazzled brilliantly, flashing like a hearty dawn every time he entered the room.

Barrett had cautiously bathed Christopher, examining him for wounds while outside the bath Hector fretted and paced. Fortunately, his initial assessment of the faun's injuries was correct; a few minor bite marks at the base of his neck, some nicks from restraining claws at his ankles and wrists, the area around his ass tender, as much from course wolf hair as multiple use. Likely, he passed out more from exhilaration and fear than from assault. Quite sure that some of the encrusted semen he had scrubbed off the limp faun came from

Christopher himself, Barrett wearily grinned in relief. The boy now slept restfully.

Actually, it was Hector that worried him most. Of the three of them, he was the oldest and most parental. Yet once the extent of the young faun's injuries had been ascertained, Hector went to his own room without a word. It was not that Barrett had a problem sitting with Christopher the whole night, but owing to Hector's nature, he had not expected to. He went to Hector's room, exhausted and hoping they might be able to watch over the recovering faun in shifts; he found him lost in a deep, troubled sleep, groaning distressfully, twisting and turning in sweat-drenched sheets. After he shut the door and wearily returned to further nurse Christopher, Barrett felt lost in a sudden sadness.

The change was upon Hector. And if Hector woke up a man, he would have to leave the apartment immediately.

The new and unmapped forest of Hector's dream was dark with unformed obstacles and unseen precipices. In the shade of invisible things, he felt as if he were churning. An indescribable sensation, as if he were afloat in an undesirable, murky sea, kicking out against something undeniable. The groans Barrett overheard were the strains of futility.

It was still dark out, when Hector awoke. Every muscle ached. At first he assumed he had a hangover, but quickly recalled that he did not drink at last night's Banquet (no faun who values his life would drink carelessly atop a skyscraper populated by werewolves). Still, his head was heavy, his vision blurred. Only when he attempted to step out of bed did he realize his transformation. As he made contact with the floor, the world spun out from under him, and he landed with a crash, pulling sweat-yellowed sheets after him. Where his hooves should have been, untried, nubile toes sprouted like dewy mushrooms atop freshly-tilled soil. Hector had shed his hooves in the night, running their dark remnants into the grease that blackened the bottom of his sheets, caked his feet like mud. Feet! They were impossibly wide, the heels tender and soft.

Hector attempted to stand but fell to his knees with such a loud thump he paused, breathless, sure the others would come running only to gasp in horror at his transformation. He examined the rest of his body; a sudden burst of black, wiry curls greedily hugged his penis. Alien tufts of hair clung to his armpits. The now dead pelt of his thighs lifted away easily by the handful. Hector wept. He had gone to bed an enchanted boy and awoke ordinary, a mere man. Exiled from the Faery Folk, his period of charmed youth had abruptly passed, unless, of course, he went with the wolves. Even then, that second

enchantment was an embrace of inner darkness, not an Arcadian joy but a sly return reliant on a formal moon.

He sat on the floor confused and mournful, relieved that the boys had not come running. Likely Barrett had dozed off while nursing Christopher. Hector pulled himself up on the side of the bed and stared down at his unsteady legs. With extreme concentration, he stood. Carefully, hesitantly, he stepped toward the bathroom. Vertigo struck. Eyes closed, he exerted control. Steadied again, he looked around the room to take stock of just how little he would have to pack.

If he were lucky, he would be able to leave before either of the boys awoke. It would be important to leave without seeing them, for becoming a man meant his desire had shifted and surely, weakened in this new state as he was, he would lust for his friends. And the idea of being inside someone, of becoming the hunter after all of these years as game, gave cause for slight arousal. He felt his newly enlarged penis blossoming at the thought. Glancing down at the tight, black springs hoarding his cock, he realized that this was something he would like to explore further in the shower.

With more resolve, keeping a hand against the wall for every new step, he made it down the hallway to the bathroom and started his bath. He stood beneath the steaming water and

tried to let his mind empty of all new worries. He looked down at the drain to see a soaked mass of flaxen fur; his thighs were now completely denuded. He marveled at the shiny new skin that was suddenly his; he had never realized his legs were so muscular, so manly. His arms seemed fuller, more defined. He ran his fingers through the tight, knotted hair entangling his lengthening penis. Closing his eyes, he imagined himself pursuing fauns. He raised his arm and licked the dark, new hair underneath. With his other hand, he surveyed the span of this new dick, its emerging scope impressive. Even by werewolf standards, he proudly thought. Happily surprised to reach the point of arousal where he needed, wanted, climaxed, Hector leaned back against the tiled wall to lose himself and allow the rising steam to erase all thoughts while he enjoyed exploring his new manhood.

That is, until Barrett briskly pulled back the grimy shower curtain.

He blushed deeply, flustered. At first, Hector turned to hide his erection, covering one foot with the other, as if it were possible to conceal his transformation from Barrett. Naked in the shower, he was now a man. Hector opened his mouth, whether to cry or shout at Barrett to leave he didn't know. But

as hot water poured across Hector's parted lips, Barrett stepped into the shower, and let the curtain fall behind him.

As water washes over Barrett he lets out a sigh, closing his eyes to let the heat renew him. Hector sees his friend with a redefined vision – as a sylvan beauty, slight nipples freshly bejeweled with water droplets, long lashes blinking slowly, heavy with water, radiant, curious eyes asking questions and answering them silently, knowingly.

Barrett puts his palms against Hector's chest. "I've known it was coming for days. I know you can't stay here Hector, but I also know I want to be your first."

His heart drums with warmth as Barrett lowers himself, surprising Hector, bypassing his throbbing cock to kneel at his feet and gently kiss his newly sculpted toes. Barrett looks up lovingly while caressing Hector's toes, nibbling at their pale undersides, eliciting pleasures of which Hector has never before imagined. Barrett's slender dick swells accordingly. The bent faun enfolds his tongue around each individual toe, reaching up as in prayer to stroke the denuded plains of Hector's strong flanks. Bliss. His eyes closed, with one hand Hector strums his rigid cock, clutching at the shower wall with the other as waves of ecstasy race up his body.

Barrett works his way up Hector's striking new form, kissing sore calves and weakened knees. As the faun licks Hector's thighs, now magnified testicles roll across his forehead. Finally, the boy pauses before his newfound shrine. He feels the head of the cock with his willing mouth, the salty tip; the hidden musk lurking within the folds of ample foreskin flood his mouth with a newly human spice. Barrett goes to the root of Hector's cock, the fresh bristle of pubic hair chafing his cheeks. Hector gasps and bucks his hips. Barrett reaches around and massages Hector's now hairless, ripe buttocks. And Hector can no longer withhold his supreme need. He pulls the faun up and faces him toward the streaming shower, hands against the wall, ample rump ready and willing.

Fumbling for the soap resting in the fogged and sullied windowsill, nearly dropping it, Hector regains his composure to expertly lather his cock. He spreads Barrett open and slaps the head of his freshly lubricated pole against the faun's ready slit. The boy exhales sharply, wagging his bottom, looking over his shoulder, giving Hector permission; they both want this. For the first time in his life, Hector pushes himself into someone else. He feels Barrett's supple bottom resist entry, he wants this resistance; new strength swirls within his gated waist, surely this cavity of warmth is his to be breached. Forced entry, water cascades down Barrett's back into their close divide, darkening

Hector's pubic mat, pooling at the bridge of flesh where they have joined. Barrett breathes deeply. Hector pulls himself nearly all of the way out only to plunge back in, eliciting a sharp cry from the faun. Leaning in to let the spray wash over his face, Barrett looks up and drinks the water pouring from Hector's mouth. They make a waterfall of their kiss. Hector grapples with his newfound control while inside the boy, trying new maneuvers, pausing to ascertain a different thrust, all of which tease out an ecstatic delight. Both feel the rush of mounting orgasm.

Hector's gyrations grow more determined and forceful as Barrett pulls at his own cock. He strikes at the boy like lightning. He rears back and cries out Barrett's name, filling the faun with hot threads of looping semen. What spills out of the boy's shattered rose dribbles down the faun's matted legs to mingle with his own cum swirling at the drain.

Hector pulled the spent, panting faun up and kissed him. They helped each other wash and then shared a thread-bare towel. When Hector stepped out of the shower his footing was steady and sure.

Chapter 9. The Ramble

A rush and a push and the land that

We stand on is ours.

It has been before.

So why can't it be now?

– The Smiths

Bill had agreed with Asterion to meet again back at Stables. Instantly, he regretted not choosing another bar, or possibly a restaurant, somewhere where Asterion would not be exposed to other, more attractive centaurs, someplace without so many flirty fauns! "Calm down," he told himself. "It's only a date. A date! Something I haven't been on in years." He looked at his reflection in the cramped bathroom mirror; he had

trimmed his beard and smoothed moisturizer onto his ruddy cheeks, giving them a healthy glow. He was wearing the new shirt he bought that afternoon – it felt stiff but looked good. The only thing left to do was go to the bar and wait for the boy.

Bill was sure he would arrive first, and deep in his heart he held that ache of possibility: What if Asterion didn't show? Flustered at his conflicting emotions, awash in anticipation and dread, Bill decided to trot over to the bar, taking the long way so as not to be too early, not to get too drunk; just in case the boy did decide to show, he wanted to be at his best.

As he slowly galloped down Seventh Avenue, Bill admired the florid pink fan of the setting sun; the burnt clouds seemed to cling to the soot-streaked Victorian apartment buildings that haughtily packed his neighborhood. He relished the thought that some of his friends might see him at Stables tonight with a cute faun on his arm, though most likely they would be off at one of their events. His friends liked to volunteer for Apples and Oats, a charity that holds auctions and raffles and silly dances, all to help supply the Fire Island centaurs in winter. Bill was quietly suspicious that they were only in it for the free T-shirts and the opportunity to meet young, earnest fauns. He never went himself. Thinking about it again, he was jealous of those centaurs stranded on Fire Island,

of the freedom to run the beaches in spring and summer, of the winters spent hibernating in ramshackle barns tucked away within the snowy thickets of Cherry Grove. And New Amsterdam offered an island life opposite of that particular paradise. You never see the sea. An island of subways you can never ride, thousands of boys you can never kiss, surrounded by skyscrapers you can never climb. Bill wondered if maybe the wrong group wasn't in receipt of charity. Likely, he just needed a stiff glass of ambrosia. Just the one. His thoughts were too heady, his expectations vacillating too much, and now he thought it better to arrive early and have a drink before the boy arrived, to calm his nerves.

Bill increased his gallop while the sun retreated past the horizon, dragging its deflated parachute of warm silky clouds after it, allowing the clear, darker hues of night to emerge.

At Stables, he nursed his drink. Thankfully none of his friends had arrived, though if Asterion was meeting him simply to say he was moving on, well then it would have him good to at least have a few of his cronies catch him in the affections of such a young buck. Bill could not tear himself away from such unnecessary thoughts. He was never a faun growing up. His change overtook him well into middle age, leaving him surprised at his own lack of self-perception and certainly

unprepared for so many things. Is anything worth this much confusion? He wondered. "This is the last one, the last boy. After tonight I'll help the guys at Apples and Oats, I'll …" But before he could finish the thought, Asterion was standing shyly at his side, stretching up on his hooves to give him a peck on the cheek. The centaur turned and blushed and smiled, and Asterion blushed back, putting his hands in Bill's, and Bill thinking, this boy really is as big as his name.

At the other end of the bar, Marcus was well into his third drink. Anxiety barely stemmed, impatiently pulling at his crotch, he once again surveyed the bar. The one decent faun, a redhead no less, was totally enraptured with some old centaur. The way things had been going of late, Marcus was surprised the place hadn't converted overnight into a troll bar. He wanted to leave but did not crave the immediate satisfaction he would find at Pluto's Basement. For some reason, he wanted to see that little faun from the other night again. If he's not here, he's probably at the Ramble, Marcus thought. And if he won't come to me, I'll come to him.

He sat upright and finished his drink. He tossed a worn dollar bill at the bar and bolted out into the night. Rushing in front of a bewildered couple about to enter a cab, he pulled the door shut before they could utter a sound. The cabdriver was a

garrulous looking satyr, horns, chipped and yellowed from age, jutted out from the tattered rim of his dull chauffeur's cap. He looked back at his impatient fare, his soup-stained billy goat's beard sweeping his shoulder, fluffy eyebrows raised in perpetual surprise at his passengers' various destinations.

"Central Park."

Ah, the satyr thought, flipping the meter. So tonight I'm Charon. Hoof to pedal, mentally plotting the right trajectory; he knew this guy was in a hurry.

They always are.

With a victorious smirk, Marcus settled back into the seat, thinking he was likely in for the ride of his life.

Inside, Bill affectionately toyed with Asterion's hair. The boy was completely naked. Again. I've got to get this boy in a shirt, Bill thought. They talked and laughed sharing Bill's ambrosia. Asterion told Bill more about his family, growing up in the suburbs, feeling like he was the only faun in town. Like so many other young fauns, he dreamed of the city. The urban sprawl of his hometown was so vast that whenever Asterion was stricken with the desire that motivates every faun, to simply frolic in the joy that is nature, he had to resort to doing

cartwheels at midnight on the local golf course. Bill laughed at this sweet image, and then gulped as the boy professed his love for Central Park. Bill blinked.

Trying to sound casual, he asked, "Do you go there at night?"

Asterion suddenly seemed nervous and looked down, scratching at one hoof with the other. "I'm allergic to werewolves, seriously," the boy earnestly stammered. "I don't really like other fauns, too, they're so silly. And men, the men remind me of why I left home."

He swallowed and paused. "Bill, I like you."

And the young faun looked up into his eyes, searching for a return on the honesty with which he had just exposed himself. It was there in Bill, a light that had always been there, waiting to be switched on, flooding out of the centaur, washing over Asterion. They kissed. And they walked out of the bar hand in hand, oblivious to everything but their mutual glow.

On the sidewalk, Bill gave Asterion an appraising look and said, "Get on top of me."

Asterion looked so shocked, Bill had to laugh. "No, no, not that way and certainly not in the street! I want to give you a ride home."

The young faun looked at Bill, gauged the seriousness of his request, nodded and leapt up, straddling the centaur's back. Bill felt his penis respond to Asterion's warm, strong buttocks parting on his spine and gave a quick gallop down the street. Happily he had rightfully judged the boy's weight. Centaurs, for all their build, cannot support as much weight as they can pull, usually only giving rides to children during the summer in Central Park. There they were granted a stretch of grassy mud to romp and frolic. Upper West Side families patiently lined up for their children to receive free rides on the backs of jolly centaurs. Small, grass-stained feet urged them to race one another, storm imaginary castles; they dutifully trotted in circles at a pace just fast enough to lift their young jockey's sun-streaked hair while still earning looks of approval from smiling but anxious parents. The centaurs ended such days spent but joyful, bedecked with woven daisy necklaces strung around their necks by appreciative children. Rarely, though, was this a service they provided dates. But tonight the air was brilliant, the breeze enchanted. Bill wanted their trot home to be something special.

With the boy steady and comfortable, he chose a more leisurely path, pointing out favorite buildings while the boy gripped the wisp of a mane at the small of his back, leaning in to better hear his commentary. Flush with a resurrected confidence, Bill felt as if the two of them were sharing the city. He was not playing host or mentor, or even simply trying to impress a date. The boy's cleaved ass straddling his back felt like an upended heart, snug, a good fit, a saddle he was all too ready to wear.

Back at Bill's apartment, the faun went back out to fetch some wine while Bill arranged the place, throwing pillows about and laying down blankets, making a more suitable nest for two, wherein he was used to sleeping alone, often with only a single pillow crushed between him and the hardwood floor. He lit some candles and waited for the boy, supine on the floor.

Asterion let himself in and gasped at the room's quick transformation. Setting himself excitedly about the kitchen, the eager faun upended some freshly cleaned glasses beside the sink and grabbed the corkscrew. Settling down in the fold of Bill's hind legs, the centaur's large, equine cock eagerly wagging in his lap, the boy nervously fumbled with the cork. Bill laughed warmly and took the bottle from Asterion to work gleaming screw into earthy cork. The faun relaxed into the centaur's hide,

stroking the rough horsehair that rippled lightly toward a bristly crest that ran the length of his stomach. Bill poured two glasses, and they toasted silently. He noticed how different the room looked, how much more intimate everything appeared under the glow of candlelight. The boy's face shone gold, each brass freckle an eternal dish of wonderment.

They looked into each other's eyes while simultaneously setting their glasses down. An enchanted kiss, the boy's nimble lips and darting tongue sparked against Bill's. He put his hands on the boy's shoulders to pull him closer, his long cock stretching to its full length beneath the faun's caresses. Neither wanted their kiss to end but both were under another, more powerful spell.

As Asterion leaned forward to embrace the ruby tip of Bill's cock, the centaur neighed, one back hoof twitching in delight. With previously un-exhibited prowess, the faun quickly rotated until his head greeted the thick, hard monster, elbows out, ass daintily in the air, easy access for Bill's exploratory tongue. With a sincere determination, the faun positioned himself on his stomach, chin to the floor, granting the cock before him as much access as possible. As Bill guided a portion of his penis into the faun's suppliant mouth he licked and kissed the boy's tender slit, still warm and sweaty from their ride

home. He plunged his tongue deeper into this moist crevice as Asterion simultaneously worked more and more of Bill's horse-cock into his mouth and throat. Bill thrust gently, wishing no harm to the lad.

While gathering the faun's buttocks in a strong grip, he carefully emptied his glass over the faun, transforming Asterion's rear into a shimmering pool of undulating wine. Lapping up the sweet, dark wine while the boy worked his cock with renewed vigor, Bill felt doubly intoxicated. Asterion slid out from his embrace and lay on the floor, thrusting his sticky buttocks up in the air. Bill stroked his beard. Surely he wanted this more than anything, but with equal measure he was afraid the very size of his cock would damage the boy. As if on cue, Asterion looked over his shoulder pleadingly.

"I can take it Bill, I know I can."

His dark pupils flashed like gems beneath long, innocent lashes, red-blonde, sweaty hair matted to his brow, the freckles racing down his back – every inch of his being begged Bill to enter him.

Bill stumbled to his feet, the sharp tap of his hooves against the hardwood floors startling the young faun. Still, he buried his face in his arms and spread his legs further. The

centaur nervously repositioned himself beside the boy, hind legs bent, fore legs straightened wide on either side of the faun's prone form, his back tense, glistening with sweat. Now his hard, ruby cock took control, salivating pre-cum across the boy's quivering buttocks; it fervently demanded entry. Bill was nearly shaking in anticipation, trying his best to exact patience from his cock. But the red snake writhed and belligerently sought admission, poking around an eager crescent. Asterion did his best to raise his rear higher, pushing his knees further out to expand and stretch his entry. And then the parting. Just the head, and the boy bit his arm to keep from screaming. Bill shuddered in ecstasy, his serious length pushing forward toward merciless rapture, hot semen drooling from the tip paying for his passage, the boy weeping openly, the centaur frightful but no longer fully in control.

They joined.

Bill neighed as he rode further into the faun. The boy arched his back, a rivulet of sweat stinging the pink rind of his distressed hole. Bill had much less than a quarter of his cock in and knew it was all the boy could take. Asterion turned his head to look at Bill, mouth agape, his cheeks red and tear-streaked, eyes unfocused, glossed with pain and ecstasy. Bill felt his orgasm mounting and struggled to remove his animal cock, but

the boy somehow held on to him from within, rising backward with the centaur to maintain the connection. He flooded the boy with an immense amount of semen, much spilled out as he withdrew to lay his heavy, spent penis across the length of Asterion's spine. The boy sighed as his own feeble orgasm leaked onto the blanket bunched beneath him. Rolling over, Bill's wet and sticky cock slapped his chest, but now they were face to face.

As they lay there, concern started to gnaw at Bill's expanding contentment. He wondered if he might have injured the faun. What if this wasn't what the boy had imagined?

Asterion noticed the gathering furrow in the centaur's brow and whispered, "That was wonderful," his face washed with tears and sweat.

They kissed. Tasting the salt of their hurricane-like encounter, in the recesses of his mind, Bill worried that such bliss is momentary at best and merely the eye of a passing storm.

Marcus had plunged rashly into the Ramble and now stood in the long shadows; the pagan night revealed all he had forgotten, all he wanted again. Fear rose in his throat as his cock furiously pushed against the restraints of his zipper. A young,

wild-eyed faun sped past him, a pack of wolves in pursuit, their hard, ruby dicks flashing between their wooly hind legs like cocked arrows targeting their prey. He could hear a werewolf breathing deeply nearby but could not see him. The rapidity of his breath made Marcus think the wolf was masturbating, or fucking a grimly silent faun. These woods held the promise of the unknown, and he was in deep.

Another frightening thought occurred to him: besides the nearly extinct pixies, werewolves and fauns were not the only Faery Folk to frequent the Ramble. Unknown to humankind, only rarely whispered of among Faery Folk, are the tatterdemalions. Roughly human-shaped wraiths, with blank faces shadowed by dirty, wide-brimmed hats pulled low, their ghostly forms were nothing more than a filthy assemblage of gray rags. They silently haunt Central Park, always alone. At a distance they seem to be nothing more than an odd constituent of the city's homeless, scouring for cans or lost in dismal thought. A closer inspection would reveal a shallow creature nothing more than rags, tattered bits of cloth adhering to one another via enchanted black filth, weary, oily venom ready to strike. With the speed of a hungry viper, it will wrap a knot of vile rag around the throat of anyone who approaches. That or the creature will take the form of an immense, angry bird, catching the wind like an unfettered kite, or looping its knotted

appendages around the nearest tree trunk, fling its billowing form up into the air, traipsing across the treetops until precious solitude is restored. Bodies made of soiled diapers, forgotten table clothes, discarded dish towels, empty, ominous hats, all imbibed with new life, or a new none-life, as if a shadow so infused with ugly stains tried to walk away from itself in disgust.

Marcus shuddered and looked around, trying hard to peer deeper into the surrounding darkness. Years ago, late one night while still a faun, tired and satiated, he took a detour he thought would lead him out of the park. The path was sparsely lit, crowded with refuse and dead branches. Shaking with fear, he had tried to make his way quickly when a mute tatterdemalion rose before him. The apparition slowly tipped his hat toward the quaking faun, revealing a fractured cloth cranium. From the dim light of the moon, he saw into its empty skull, a bowl of nothingness sewn together by cobwebs and dust. The mere recollection frosted his spine.

"And there's no way I'll recognize that little faun from the other night in this darkness. What was I thinking?" But Marcus knew he wasn't thinking, nor was it the alcohol; he had not had that much to drink. Instinct and desire had lured him into the park. And now that he was here, he felt frozen, sober,

enveloped by every treacherous freedom the Ramble embodied. Nervously, he unzipped his pants and hesitantly pulled out his demanding cock, as if even exposing it to this atmosphere would somehow draw him further in. And it did. As his penis more fully engorged, a fearful faun leapt into the shadows where Marcus had secreted himself. The faun froze as pursuing wolves passed by. Marcus could smell the rich dampness of earth tilled by claw and hoof. Sensing the young creature's fear and knowing no stronger aphrodisiac, Marcus stepped forward and grabbed the sweaty faun. The trembling boy surrendered without a struggle. Collapsing willingly before his grip, perhaps the boy felt a man was naturally gentler than a wolf. How wrong. Marcus quickly pushed the boy to his knees, demanding immediate service. The boy tried to ease the angry cock pulsing before him into his mouth, but Marcus would not have it, and thrusted furiously at the surprised but unlocked lips. The boy knew not to cry out in protest for the woods were thick with werewolves in the height of their hunger.

Looking up at his captor with pleading eyes, his long lashes braided with tears, knees caked with black soil, the faun slavishly worked the cock in his mouth. In this private night behind curtained eyes, the tongue cradling his cock was nearly the warmth Marcus required. Nearly. He was not patient enough to allow the faun to dispense the full lubrication required to ease

his impending assault. With a quick grunt to signal both satisfaction and completion, he uprooted his cock while pushing the boy further to the ground with his foot. The boy, stunned, sensed he should now offer up his rear to the man towering above and positioned himself, elbows anchored against the chilly ground, for the coming mount. Marcus spread the boy's supple buttocks, twisting the ridge of his fist against pink crevice, knuckling the opening in preparation, the tiny pucker tightening in fear as the bulbous head of his cock hovered near the alarmed slit. The faun's self-imposed silence filled him with exhilaration; he felt powerful, like the wolf devouring the submissive faun in the bushes nearby. Marcus plunged his barely-lubed cock all the way in. Feeling the boy's resistance collapse beneath him, feeding off his youthful heat, he plundered the faun, pushing himself further and further in at a furious pace. In total surrender, the faun sighed beneath the onslaught, his tear-streaked face flat on the ground, his thin, brittle arms turned out in total supplication to the enveloping pleasure and pain. Marcus rode the boy into the dirt.

As his orgasm built, he slowed, rhythmically priming the faun, pulling his cock nearly all the way out, again plunging deeply, his tight, lower abdominal muscles audibly striking the sweaty buttocks spread beneath him. Marcus brought his hands to his head as his surging load flooded the boy; the faun

whimpered and groveled in total satisfaction as his own cream unfurled, a bitter unction lost in a curlicue of mud.

Spent, he pushed himself out of the faun and stood, panting, delirious with pleasure and a rising arrogance.

A man among wolves, he had stalked the Ramble and brought down a faun. He stood naked, clothed only in darkness; the faun kissed his feet in unreserved gratitude before scampering into the brush. Now Marcus was alone. A creeping uncertainty struck; he was unsure where exactly he was in the shadowy labyrinth of the Ramble. Would the nearest path lead toward an exit or deeper into the thicket? He knelt and stealthily felt about for his jeans and jacket, hoping to regain his bearings. He could not find his clothes. Nearby a werewolf bayed, then another.

Now the hunter would be the hunted until he made his way safely to the street.

Asterion moved about the room, blowing out the candles one by one. Bill lay on his side, admiring the boy's efforts. He was also wishing for more wine, but found himself too sleepy and instead desired for the boy to settle in his arms. It was too soon to start reviewing the evening's activities, but Bill couldn't help it. It had been a long time since he had gone that far with

someone, even longer since he had gone that far with someone he cared about.

He watched as Asterion gently washed the wine glasses in the sink. And just as Bill's sleepiness announced itself with a long, leonine yawn, Asterion presented himself for a kiss goodnight.

"I must be going, Bill."

Bill was startled awake. "Stay the night! It's terribly late, and I just realized, I don't even know where you live," he stammered, blinking at the boy. Though he hoped not to come off as too desperate, the look on his face clearly said, "Stay."

Asterion put his arm around Bill and whispered in his ear, "I'd love to, when it's the right time."

He fingered the centaur's slight beard as they kissed, Bill weakly patted his bare bottom. Asterion let himself out as Bill drifted off to sleep, drowsy but not content.

Marcus was scared. For an hour, he had tried to make his way out of the Ramble. As he wound through paths thick with sexual treachery twice he had hurried in the direction of a light that hopefully emanated from the street, each time finding the same lone crooked lamp post planted firmly in the heart of

the Ramble, its faint light pallid yellow, sparsely illuminating the well-trodden trail. In the shadows, a pack of wolves encircled two trembling fauns. By the glint of their tiny horns, he thought they might be the two he'd had at Pluto's Basement. This was confirmed by their familiar cries of joy and pain as he hurried past. He knew he was hopelessly lost and believed he was being followed. I don't want this, he thought.

Naked, defenseless, Marcus was desperate to escape but felt he should move through the brush as quietly as possible, hoping the presence he sensed behind him was nothing more than the projection of his own very real fear. He came around a large boulder and froze: a very large werewolf lay atop the form of a splayed faun. Strong, taut furry buttocks tightened, it's back arched. Marcus guessed the wolf's considerable length was buried deep in the violated ass of the beautiful faun. The boy was completely still, transfixed by the painful ecstasy generated from the werewolf. The wolf, intent on his building orgasm, was oblivious to Marcus. He forgot his fear and frustration as his cock stirred. Kneading his dick as the werewolf and faun slowly fucked, he could sense the wolf's long pole rhythmically slipping in and out of the passive boy. He feverishly pulled on his now fully engorged cock, masturbating at the quiet intensity before him when the werewolf stopped and stared right at him. Swiftly the creature withdrew from the confused faun, who also

gazed at Marcus, but with a look of sudden terror. Marcus thought to run, but the werewolf promptly merged with the forest without a sound, abandoning the now whimpering faun.

Momentarily confused, he wondered if he had somehow scared the wolf off. No, that's impossible, he thought. A new fear filled him. In the deep silence of the night Marcus listened.

Beside his own ragged breath and that of the lightly sobbing faun, he detected a deep, steady rhythm over his shoulder. He turned. A tremendous wolf surveyed the park from atop a moon-scarred rock. Hair hung off his long arms in stiff clumps twisting to points as sharp as wicked swords; with every breath his long, lupine muzzle parted to reveal a crop of fiery teeth. An impossibly long cock twitched malevolently between his legs; this monstrosity hung heavy, as if weighted by an iron fist reaching for the ground. The thing was as thick as Marcus' arm, and equally jointed, bending just past the parting of black foreskin to lengthen another ten inches. With a wet snap, the hideous penis demonstrated its strength while extending itself lethally in Marcus' direction. With trepidation, Marcus was drawn to the werewolves' eyes, red cathedrals of hunger. Bane himself had marked him for prey.

Bane.

So every frightening Faery Tale was true.

Bane the Hunter stalked the Ramble in numerous tales, too many tales, the young Marcus and so many of the faun brood had thought, to actually be true. But along with the ferocity of his slaying cock, so too were his red, red eyes well-known. Every story about Bane began with those piercing eyes and usually ended with a bone crushing bite as he brought his victims down for a bloody orgy of violence; his preference for men and other werewolves was also legendary (as fauns would not generally survive such an onslaught long enough to afford him an agreeable fuck).

How useless to run, but the terror Marcus felt was divorced from all rationality, and so he ran, sprinting over the cowering boy to cut a path through the dark woods. The Hunter Bane paused and stretched his arms behind him while thrusting his pelvis forward, to give his demon cock a false stab toward its prey before bounding over the now-fainted-faun, hard on the human's trail.

Crossing the Great Lawn, Marcus prayed for his life. Sprinting beneath the moonlight naked, in such an open area he felt terribly exposed, but at every turn within the Ramble he had to dodge a branch, scramble over a sudden out-cropping of rock. Every time he slowed, the claws behind him noisily

shredded foliage and a shower of leaves propelled him forward. Now, however, he no longer heard the werewolf in pursuit. Too fearful to stop, too fearful to look back, Marcus realized he had reached the Great Lawn's center, from which he could see the rise of apartment buildings to the west. The street. If I reach the street I might just survive. He stopped, out of breath, and dropped to a crouch. The werewolf was nowhere to be seen.

"Surely he's still stalking me. So far he's only been playing with me. Probably he's waiting for me on the western-most edge, knowing I'd go for the street."

Suddenly a skipping faun, not too far off, interrupted his thoughts. As the lone faun crossed the field, Marcus hoped this would divert the wolf's attentions.

"No. It's me he wants. Just surrender."

Suddenly tired, he thought about lying down to await his fate. The faun slipped into the black woods. Alone again. The grass shone a resilient blue in the moonlight. No, I've got to get to the street. Having caught his breath, he decided to make a run for the street, no matter how futile it might seem. At that moment, one of the low hills that made up the lawn seemed to shift. Marcus froze. Two red eyes appeared. The werewolf Bane arose and was upon him. Striding up to Marcus with all the

assurance of the hunter who knows that his prey is all but consumed, Bane stood proudly, allowing a fearful Marcus to examine him. The pungent musk coming off the werewolf was overpowering; he swooned and fell to his knees, the beast's stench dank, hypnotic, the sweat steaming from his feral chest and balls a dizzying fog of enticement. And danger.

Marcus was appalled; his cock was stirring, an unfamiliar ache pulsed, at first weakly, then with the full conviction of a growing hunger, deep within his bare buttocks. Suddenly he yearned for the coming attack as much as he dreaded it. As the gigantic wolf stepped more clearly into view, Marcus could make out his towering penis, ominous in the moonlight. It rose like a malevolent whip about to strike. He whimpered, mesmerized by the finger-like veins that gripped the werewolf's rising cock, fusing at the head into a red, blunt weapon that seethed and throbbed. It was a blind, angry force. This hell-forged hammer, sensing prey cowering before it, bent at its sick joint to slap Marcus across the face. Stunned, Marcus wavered, slack-jawed, while the werewolf grasped him roughly by the hair, pushing the beast-cock against his lips. The pre-cum smeared across his face had a harsh sulfuric smell that burned his lips. In vain he struck out at the beast and then lunged wildly toward the Ramble. The monster grasped him by the ankle and violently yanked him back. As punishment, he raked Marcus'

chest with his claws and fresh crimson cuts stung in the cool night air. The werewolf glowered, crouching to inspect his victim; Marcus was again overcome as the harsh stench rising from between the wolf's flanks enveloped him. Bane sniffed curiously at Marcus's lengthening penis, so slight and tiny compared to his own proud bludgeon; he turned his human quarry over roughly. Grasping Marcus by the thigh, he parted his kicking form, one claw easily encircling an entire leg. He inserted a dry, jagged black nail into a very unwilling slit. Marcus let out a cry of pain while the wolf howled in satisfaction and began working another knife-like finger mercilessly into his resistant hole.

Marcus clawed at the earth, straining against this violation while his traitor cock stretched at the unequaled pleasure spreading through his body. The hot breath of the werewolf at his ear kept him from total elation, however. There was no kindness in the steely claws working his buttocks. Without warning, the wolf's cock cut at his backside, the raw mass of muscle tunneling toward his very sanity. He gasped as the unusual gristle of the werewolf's cock raked his besieged hole. The ragged panting at his ear increased as Bane bucked with hostile fervor. Wild-eyed, Marcus gripped the ground beneath him to steady himself against the onslaught; he knew if he displeased this monster in the least he would be maimed or

killed. Yet part of him was opening to this new pleasure as every stab echoed in his own now-rigid cock. The wolf's grunting ceased. Dazed, Marcus weakly tried to brace himself for the next round of torture. With a brutal slap, he was spun on his back. Bane pulled his legs further apart and forcefully re-entered him, the dirt and grit now adhering to his wild cock an added traction. Marcus went slack, arms out, head back, exposing the tender white flesh of his neck. With a mighty howl Bane forced his cock in deeper while sinking his fangs into ripe flesh. Marcus exhaled as blood flowed down his chest, a crimson blanket of expanding warmth. The molten rod that filled him further engorged as the werewolf deepened his bite. He could feel sharp teeth knocking at his shoulder blade and struggled against the jaws that gripped him. Suddenly, the warmth of his own blood, the internal heat of the cock within him, the brightness of fear, everything coalesced, giving rise to a new level of awareness. Calmness washed over him. Peacefulness. The constant circle of carnivore and prey tightened further until it closed around his heart.

Bane supped on his neck, lost in his own impending orgasm, the sweat that gathered on his hairy muzzle dripped into the wound of his feast. And Marcus felt the initial spark of a mounting change. The wolf rhythmically rocked himself in and out of Marcus' now forgiving hole. As Bane's grip on his

victim's neck relented, more blood pulsed out to paint his chest and abdomen red. The monster howled deeply, total satisfaction rumbled throughout his body as he pumped Marcus with charging sperm. And Marcus could feel new life wildly coursing through him, cementing his new identity beneath the haze of pain and passion. The change will come. The werewolf pulled his slick cock out quickly and turned, sniffed at the wind, then crept off toward the Ramble. He would likely feast three more times before dawn. A wind arose, trees clamored in a rush of futility while the stars burrowed further into their dark habits.

Marcus lay on his stomach, his buttocks encrusted with a sick lather of sperm and blood. A balm of moonlight soothed the wound at his neck and shoulder. The mantle of heat that encased him had yet to dissolve; if anything it was solidifying, the amber of a new, freshly minted destiny.

He was naked and thirsty. Dawn was still several hours away. He stood, every muscle aching. The moon was steady, huge, gloriously pocked with indifference. And for the first time he heard the night. The grass rebounding beneath him rowdy and elastic, the dry whistle of the breeze combing the trees sounded like a thousand brass coins tumbling down a marble staircase of infinite length. He could hear fauns giggling a mile

away. He shook with anticipation as a new sense of clarity filled his mind.

I can't wait to taste them all.

Chapter 10. Mermaids Never Wave Goodbye

Never love a statue.

– Maecenas

Christopher awoke feeling weak but rested. His jaw ached and his buttocks felt like the battered-yet-sturdy hull of an overly-raided pirate ship. Barrett was still asleep at his bedside, twisted among blankets. A spilt cup of tea stained the warped floorboards at his hooves. Famished, Christopher went to the kitchen to forage, thinking he really should buy the groceries this week, that he relied on his roommates for so much, they even did the shopping. Just a few months ago, he had come by bus to Port Authority with nothing but the knapsack on his back. He had known that Faery Folk congregated on Eighth Avenue, and embarrassingly enough,

used a compass to help find the way. He saw a posting for a room for rent taped to an Eighth Avenue bus stop, called the number listed from a payphone, and within a few minutes Hector was interviewing him over a cup of coffee. The interview quickly turned toward a mentorship of sorts, as Hector spent most of the afternoon escorting him around Chelsea, walking in and out of restaurants until they had found Christopher a job waiting tables at a microscopic Village café, Elysian Pancakes, his high school French just passable enough to add that needed flair to the daily specials. It wasn't until weeks later that he realized their apartment building on Ninth Avenue was the focal point of faun-life. Though his roommates teased him good-naturedly, they had done more than simply initiate him into the life of New Amsterdam Faery Folk; they had made the adventure a journey.

After stuffing himself with berries and a slice of stale bread unearthed from behind an expired carton of milk, he went to Hector's room while water for his tea boiled. He wanted to thank Hector for shepherding him safely through last night and that, though the lurid memories of the Banquet still fogged his mind, to tell him he was feeling fine.

Hector's room was bare. The bed was stripped of sheets, the closet door stood open to reveal a few gaunt wooden hangers and nothing more.

Christopher ran to wake Barrett while the teakettle gave a shrill start before launching into a full screech.

Hector spent the afternoon at the Metropolitan Museum, self-conscious of how quiet his now-human footsteps sounded. He dearly missed the echo of himself. Docents in stiff navy blazers used to give him sour looks as the clap of his hooves reverberated throughout the galleries. Now his feet felt both cushioned and constricted, confined in sneakers purchased from a Times Square street vendor with the last of his money. But here, here was sanctuary. Without his friends' knowledge, he had spent many afternoons in the museum, wandering the halls, finding his own peace away from Faery life, seemingly far from the Ramble, just outside the walls, beyond the hustle of waiting tables in a cramped restaurant, the faun-filled apartment building.

He had been in a frenzy to leave the apartment before the boys woke. Though they slept soundly in Christopher's room, Hector quickly grew to understand all too well why men and faun do not live together: their cramped apartment was rank with the previously undetectable musk of three fauns; he had

137

been in a constant state of arousal since shedding his faundom, his rigid penis throbbing painfully for release every second he remained in the apartment. Throwing his few clothes into a backpack, he filled a brown grocery bag with trifles and toiletries. From the street, he had gazed up at the window he used to look out of. The light from the window above already shone like that of a distant star. He knew he could never reach it again, but wished to remain in its orbit for as long as possible.

He didn't have that much money, so he nursed a single drink at Stables until closing time and slept on a bench somewhere in the village; the memory of Barrett's kisses kept him warm, though his heart was heavy as he thought about his friends back at the apartment. He hoped Christopher was doing okay. Hector had yet to really think about where he would live. Last night was a nice summery evening, but that was no excuse – he needed to find somewhere to stay very soon. He did not have to work tonight and was in no mood to hang out at Stables again; the thought of Pluto's Basement made him shudder.

Too many thoughts darkened his mood, which, typically, was why he came to the Museum. Here he could ascend a staircase and enter another time period, turn a corner and encounter a painting of the utmost serenity, or a portrait of a fiery persona, centuries dead, challenging still, with the liveliest

eyes, either the mirror of his disposition or the antidote to his problems. Hector never brought his faun friends to the museum, though now if he were to do so it would be on a date, a concept too peculiar to entertain at the moment. He looked up to note that he was in the African galleries. Perfect. He was not too far from his favorite gallery, Greek and Roman Sculpture. If he felt free to wander without a care in the other rooms of the museum, this was the one place where he found himself. Or, to put it more succinctly, in this room Hector found that he was in love.

Busts with broken noses crowded one corner, a silent senate glaring at the statues of emperors and Gods; few were full-bodied, some with pilfered genitals, others missing an arm, all relatively intact on their daises, gaze permanently fixed somewhere above the heads of flushed tourists and awed students shuffling past. All but one. The statue of Antinous always confidently returned his look of longing. The perfect prize of the Metropolitan's collection, Hector had memorized the tale of his short life engraved on the small brass plate beside his statue: Antinous, renowned for his beauty, young consort to the Roman Emperor Hadrian, murdered or accidentally drowned as the lovers took a romantic journey down the Nile nearly two thousand years ago. If it was murder it was at the hands of the emperor's enemies. Hadrian mourned the loss with a ferocity that pressed the boy into the heavens, marking him a

New God, giving rise to a city in Egypt that bore his name, to numerous cults and, eons later, statues of exquisite refinement, known throughout the modern world as the pinnacle of sculpture, the final precipice of a culture about to mark its decline with the ugly advent of Christianity.

The figure before Hector was one of flawless, masculine grace. Countless times, when the guards were distracted or napping, Hector furtively caressed his smooth thighs. The pure white marble shone brilliant and virile in the stream of afternoon sun flooding through the skylight. Naked save an Egyptian headdress, Antinous seemingly regarded him with similar, impossible desire. Only today Hector needed more than a stolen caress.

When the room was relatively free from tourists and he had checked to make sure no guards were watching, he reached over to hold the young god's hand. The eyes of Antinous were pupil-less, two lofty, milk-filled orbs. Far from foreboding, they were calm galaxies in which Hector wished to swim. Every splash would ignite a wave of new suns and effervescent planets with smoky rings and silky opal moons; the wake of his backstroke would ripple across constellations.

The Werewolves of Central Park

He could tell from the arc of the late afternoon light that dusk was near. Just beyond the ancient sculpture galleries the long dining hall was nearly empty of patrons, exhausted busboys in bowties busily prepared for closing time. Many of the restaurant workers had already left for the day, leaving the expansive dining room mostly deserted, tables already set for the next day's bustle; crisp, thick muslin tablecloths draped low, reaching the floor. Hector thought of how amazing his perfect lover must look in the moonlight.

Bill woke too early to fret the day away. Where he should have been content with last night's date, he was mildly annoyed that Asterion did not stay the night. Something about the boy's departure just did not seem right. He worried such thoughts would prematurely sabotage the relationship, laughing to himself that he would even label their encounters a "relationship" in his mind. Still, he thought, the way we look each other, the way we talk about things, that's real. Yes, it was real. And that was the reason Bill was cleaning the apartment for the second time this morning, going so far as to alphabetize the weathered paperbacks on the mantle. He was doing everything he could to avoid the kind of thoughts that occur all too naturally among Faery Folk. "Of course it's real between us, just like it's real between him and someone else. He doesn't stay the night, hasn't told me about where he lives because he

lives with another centaur, likely one who's done better for himself than a crappy studio apartment with a fireplace that doesn't work."

Eventually Bill realized that he could not battle such thoughts within the claustrophobic environs of his now overly-tidied home. He pulled on a fresh shirt and sped out, down the street toward the piers.

When he first moved to the city, he took solace in walking along the piers. Many men cruised there late at night, looking to trick with Faeries on the outskirts of the city, far from other human eyes. Even then, Bill preferred the mornings. Lining the highway, the abandoned, fractured warehouses washed in the smooth light of dawn somehow seemed content in their uselessness. And with the city behind him, he could look out across the Hudson River and let the peaceful solitude of its waters sooth him. His only company was the occasional mermaid, surfacing to wave a lithe, emerald arm in greeting. Bill always vigorously waved back. With a splash, she would submerge again, and if it was a late summer day like this morning, likely head south toward a winter job in some Florida theme park. Nowadays, sleek lofts have replaced the dilapidated warehouses; mermaids were not often sighted anymore.

Bill still enjoyed a morning trot. Really, he was only comfortable coming here at the earliest possible hour; otherwise annoyed bicyclists raced past, glaring back at him over their shoulders, and mothers with strollers rushed to the curb as if he were a wild beast. Bill halted at the sea wall. The brown water was calm, broken only by the wake of beleaguered tugboats riding low in the river. He had heard a mermaid or two still worked a casino in Atlantic City, trapped in some cramped restaurant aquarium, forever performing somersaults for slack-jawed Midwesterners. Moments like this he was inclined to think less disparagingly of the Fire Island centaurs. Maybe they were right in creating a sanctuary. Certainly no man is an island, but doesn't living on one allow you to draw upon such characteristics? At that thought Bill turned to watch two pert fauns jog past, beautiful buttocks bobbing in unison, their shoulders glistening with earnest sweat. A woman with a wide stroller spotted him, shot him a damning look and veered dramatically to the other side of the path, as if he might rear up, unprovoked, to trample the drooling little dumpling bundled before her. Bill smiled. No, not if that island is New Amsterdam. He decided to trot over to Union Square and buy some apples and fresh celery to stew for tonight's dinner.

Turning his back on the river, he crossed the highway, allowing himself to trot perhaps a bit too close to the woman

with the stroller, so that his friendly neigh rattled the poor dear, her purse and cell phone flying into traffic. Bill smiled but didn't dare turn his head to catch the withering expression surely screwed on her face; he was wondering if he had enough cinnamon back at the apartment. Stewed apples are nothing without cinnamon.

Marcus made it home sometime after dawn, having scoured the Ramble for some other wolf's discarded jeans. Wolf. In the shower, he ran his fingers over the freshly-healed lacerations that dotted his shoulder. The white brail tingled beneath his touch. He let water fill his open mouth and pour out. His muscles felt new, everything had a deeper scent. He walked naked from the shower and collapsed on the bed and immediately fell into a deep, nourishing sleep.

Marcus dreamt of the Great Lawn, now borderless, without the harsh, unnecessary hem of streets. No apartment buildings, no traffic. And here, he ran and ran, spirited claws upturning earth. Now he was part of the pack. His brothers ran alongside him, offering encouraging nips at his flanks, baring their teeth in a show of admiration. He was strong, leaping over rock formations, flighty fauns scurrying away as fast as they could. He knew the one he wanted, lifting the sweet musk off the faun's buttocks while still a mile away, savoring the living

perfume simmering in his snout, the night air a broth of scents; he will be able to single this one out and follow him throughout the Ramble no matter how long the pursuit lasts. And chasing the faun, with every leap the hunger in him built, pulsing through his re-forged cock, now red and steaming in the night, an angry bullet racing toward the bull's-eye secreted within the buttocks of a frightened faun. And in this dreamworld, Marcus realized his thirsts had always been this uncast bullet, until the bite of Bane gave it shape.

As he stretched and purred in bed, the wolf-form nestling inside him roared through the endless night of his mind.

Chapter 11. Life Is No Faery Tale

Why am I going out of my head,

Whenever you're around?

The answer is obvious ...

Love has come to town.

– The Talking Heads

Marcus examined himself in the mirror. Newly emerging stabs of white hair at his temples shocked him, yet instead of making him look older they gave him a more feral quality, highlighting how dark and full his hair was otherwise. The other changes were more subtle. His calves felt like rocks and looked higher, as if he were built to pounce. Foreskin hung heavy from his cock, a thick holster to a deadly weapon. His

dick twitched, eager for the hunt. The hunt. Marcus couldn't wait to get to the park. He had slept through the afternoon without bothering to call work; when he awoke, it was nearly twilight. He rushed to get dressed. At the door, he paused and looked back toward his disheveled bed. No longer will I have to spend hours enticing young fauns back to that bed. From now on, I'll take what I want from the Ramble. In fact, this is no longer an apartment, it's a lair. He smiled at the thought, leaping down the steps two at a time until he made the street. Hailing a cab, he smiled again when the cabdriver asked, "Destination?"

"Central Park." He repeated last night's incantation to the driver. As they wove slowly through traffic, Marcus settled assuredly into his seat.

Pulling at his hungry cock through his jeans, he watched as skyscrapers blazed with the setting sun, the thin flashes on mirrored glass winking across mute obelisks. By the time they reached Columbus Circle, he could no longer contain himself and, as the taxi idled in traffic, Marcus tossed a crumpled twenty at the driver and leapt out of the cab. Jumping the low stone wall of the park, Marcus stopped to breathe in the rich, dark bouquet of the coming night; the air was already laced with the sweet scent of faun. And other werewolves. He was

surprised to find their earthy musk equally enticing. His crotch thickened at the thought of joining the pack. His arms and thighs ached, ready for the change. He rushed toward the Ramble before the shift overtook him, making him a menace to the centaur-drawn carriages already eager to withdraw from the park.

Passing the fountain, he noticed the moon looming large in the sky, a prescient force. Already, from across the pond he could make out the figures of other restless men, lurking about, impatient for the change. He sprinted over the footbridge and ran into the thick shadows of the Ramble. The aroma of cum-soaked earth nearly brought the wolf out of him. He shook with potent ecstasy as newfound sensations rocked his body. He caught the scent of a faun that had probably taken this path over an hour ago, yet his scent glowed in Marcus' flaring nostrils. And so taken with the scent, he plunged further into the woods, stripping off his shirt as a dark raven of hair coarsened across his chest. He paused, wild with lust, concentrating his last human thoughts on the act of pulling off his shoes and pants, stashing them beneath a tree and fixing the spot in his mind for morning, when he would regrettably resume human shape.

He parted his lips to reveal long, dagger-like teeth. As the wolf inside him swallowed the last portion of his human

soul, he let out such a howl that his brethren immediately joined in; the trees rung with the sounds of righteous hunger. His ample penis sprung from between his legs fully engorged, an angry red sword ready to flay the backside of the nearest faun. His eyes were burning telescopes, his ears lengthened and sharpened to points; fur from his chest spread down to his crotch, clutching his testicles in a hot pelt. The hair across his thighs thickened as well; his entire body was covered in a wonderful, sleek new fur. He cut the air with shiny black claws and shook in wonderment. As the last delicate tendril of the sun withdrew, he could see everything. He could smell everything. He could hear everything. And within the light symphony of the forest, he detected the separate heartbeats of over a dozen fauns. From the web of a thousand living scents, he could pluck the strands of these fauns and follow the invisible threads that were wafting and winding throughout numerous trails. The heat of his animal brothers pulsed in his vision; werewolves were everywhere around him. Those nearest sensed his unbridled ferocity, the un-honed instincts of a new wolf. Many werewolves were attracted by such a nascent display of instinct and approached, their cocks thickening before them in anticipation of initiating a new recruit into their brotherhood. Marcus was instantly aware of the surrounding wolves and broke out toward the nearest trail. Soon he caught the scent of

the closest faun. He envisioned the supple buttocks: warm, moistened with sweat from a romp across the Great Lawn, the juices within the faun's hole a perfect marinade for the very rape he wished to inflict, the very thought of which brought forth a new surge of hunger within his cock.

Marcus leapt forward, bounding down the path, nearly on all fours in pursuit of his prey. The unseen faun heard his bestial crashing and took off in a fast sprint. The hunt was on. He roared through the woods. Foliage flashed by, the heat of his brother wolves trailed behind him like sizzling comets as he hurled toward his prey. Fresh instinct dawned: this prey will only be his when offered. The faun must ultimately submit. He will capture the boy, for sure. But for Marcus the end of the hunt is defined by a previously un-sensed surrender, the faun giving himself freely at the end of the pursuit is the true goal, and with this knowledge Marcus slowed his pace, not enough to lose the trail of the faun, but enough to make it more a dance, a dance through the maze of trees and twilight-bespeckled rock. With his new form came new revelations. Here, in the center of the park, courtships of the night progressed with an animal stealth illuminated by a moon supreme.

Hector stepped out from beneath the dining room table, shivering in the cool stillness of the vast museum. He wanted to

run through the halls and galleries, arms outstretched, basking in the solitude of the private universe now at his disposal. But this universe was not entirely free from danger; museum guards lurked malevolently (or so Hector imagined) about. He had waited beneath the table quite some time before emerging, timing their rounds until he was sure he could be alone with Antinous. The museum, when so empty, reverberating with the steps of any approaching guard, giving him more than enough time to again seek sanctuary beneath the table.

While huddling under the table, Hector had shed his clothes. Still uncomfortable in pants and shoes, he craved the natural nudity of his recent past. As he strode confidently toward Antinous, the moonlight bouncing dark ribbons from the skylight across his bare chest and naked thighs, he passed the familiar sentinels that kept him company and wondered if they, too, were filled with silent love. Standing before the statue, Hector suddenly felt flush with embarrassment; his entertaining fantasy had meandered into a likely misdemeanor. Though staying past closing is probably not the same as breaking and entering, it was likely illegal; midnight nudity in the Metropolitan was an entirely different matter. He sighed, overtaken by a sense of futility. The statue before him represented everything in life likely not found atop a corresponding pedestal. Nothing is that perfect, that easy. A

saying often wryly repeated among Faery Folk is that "Life is no Faery Tale." Indeed. Wearily trying to muster up some amount of dignity, Hector thought to at least let his fantasy run its course. He raised himself up on his toes to kiss his motionless lover good-bye.

He never expected Antinous to kiss back.

At first he was unsure if fantasy alone provided the cool response that brushed his lips, but then the sure marble hand of the statue gently held him as he collapsed, falling into the embrace of a dream suddenly alive.

Asterion had obviously enjoyed the dinner Bill had prepared. Stifling a cinnamony belch, the young faun stretched and yawned among the pillows on the floor, claiming sincere astonishment over the number of dishes derived from apples. Their evening together had progressed perfectly. Instead of meeting at Stables, they met at the piers and walked along the waterfront. Bill could tell that Asterion was relieved by the change of venue. As a country boy he savored the outdoors, the fresh air.

Back at his apartment, Bill made dinner for the boy, allowing him to help stir the apples. Together they set a romantic picnic, replete with a red-checkered tablecloth Bill had

salvaged from the back of his miniscule closet. Asterion now dozed peacefully, head resting on a battered pillow, arm across one of Bill's thick, folded legs. Bill admired the rapid yet restful rise and fall of the faun's slight chest; legs parted casually, his buoyant, tiny cherubic penis relaxed below a smooth, full belly.

Bill caressed Asterion's reddish-blonde locks. "Stay the night," he asked.

A palpable uneasiness rose up from within the boy. Asterion stared at the ceiling for a full minute. "Thank you, Bill, I'd love to, but really, I must go. I've got to get up early tomorrow." The sincerity in his voice sounded forced.

Bill felt as if he'd said something wrong. But no, he thought, this is completely natural. "Why shouldn't we be together? I'm not asking too much, to wake up next to my lover, am I?" But the pleading look in the boy's eyes gave Bill pause, and he refrained from expressing his obvious reaction. He kissed Asterion lightly. The boy gratefully reciprocated, but he knew this was their kiss goodnight, wherein he was more than ready for a kiss good morning.

After Asterion shut the door behind him, Bill knew he would be unable to sleep. A flicker of desperation struck his mind and caught fire; he rose, paused a moment to give the faun

enough time to make it to the street, then, steeling himself against an action that could very well doom their budding relationship, Bill left his apartment to follow the boy.

Hector was understandably amazed. Actually, he was somewhere past amazed, beyond bewildered, scared, aroused, nor even suspicious that the medieval madness of certain paintings in the Metropolitan had infected his mind. So many emotions, all subsumed by one: Hector was, above all else, in awe.

Antinous stepped down from his marble pedestal. Marble. Hector hesitantly caressed the skin of his cool embracer; hard, smooth and frightfully pale. The strength of mountains carved into human form. He was being held by a man of stone.

Antinous smiled. "Do not be afraid."

Hector opened his mouth to reply but could not think of anything to say. This symbol of perfection, a vessel his imagination had filled with everything he had ever wanted in a man, spoke, spoke a command, breaking one spell while casting so many others.

"Do not be afraid," he repeated with a voice firm and deep, as if resonating from within some ancient temple. "I have enjoyed our time together. I was surprised to see you this evening, and this afternoon I was very surprised to see you have become a man. You make a very handsome man," Antinous playfully patted one of Hector's thighs.

He began to calm down. Gathering himself together, he asked a single question.

"How?"

Antinous loosened his embrace and, taking him by the hand, walked with Hector through the sculpture gallery. "I am no replica, I am Antinous. Many at Hadrian's court were jealous of me, of our perfect love. On the morning of my birthday, I stood upon the deck of our ship, admiring the fertile shores of the Nile, when an evil magician, secreted among the slaves by those who wished to supplant me, came from behind whispering a hex that made me a statue, a horrible Pygmalion in reverse! And with a sinister laugh he pushed me overboard where I sank, if you will forgive, how do you say it … the pun? Where I sank like a stone."

Hector blinked and squeezed the impossibly strong hand holding his and asked the obvious question. "But how?"

"Well, my love, then I was alone. Oh how I wished I could have cried. The Nile would have flooded with my tears. Alone in the darkness, I thought that this must be death. I thought this must be worse than death. Did you know that being alone for so long means running out of dreams? I ran out of dreams. I missed my lover for one hundred years. I plotted my revenge on those long dead for another hundred years. I ran through the labyrinth of mad philosophies in my mind for several hundred more before I was recovered in the nets of a fisherman."

They walked hand in hand among the graven busts of philosophers and emperors.

"Oh the light of day! Again, my tears would have salted the Nile if I were not stone! And as a statue I could stare into the sun without risking blindness. Let me tell you, after a thousand years of darkness I feasted on the light. But still, I could not move, not speak. I was a prisoner in my own body."

Antinous paused before the serene, knowledgeable bust of his former lover Hadrian. Reaching across centuries for a farewell long-ago robbed of him, he caressed his bearded check with a forlorn familiarity. Certain sadness blew across the face of the living statue. Hector was silent, respectful of all that

Antinous endured, still stunned to be holding a hand made of marble. And liking it. After a moment they moved on.

"These happy peasants sold me to the invader Napoleon, and I was moved with the treasures of his court across Europe. The feasts I witnessed! In Rome we dined with austerity, I promise you that. And that corrupted language. I thought I had been seized by a race of mad birds. But slowly, I began to discern a Latin word or two. Frozen there, I absorbed a wholly new world. My gods were gone, my empire dust, though nothing of men had changed. With the fall of Napoleon, I ended up in many private collections, landing in a dark box one day that recalled my watery tomb, only to be unpacked and placed in this museum in time for its grand opening, nearly one hundred years ago."

They stopped before an armless Athena; Hector was even more surprised that they were the same height. He felt Antinous' perfect, firm biceps, then put his palms against the statue's chest.

"I can feel your warmth," Antinous said. "Your kiss lifted my curse, in part. Black magic is always countered by white magic. If I had not felt for you the way you feel for me, I would still be frozen on that pedestal."

And they embraced. Kissing deeply, Antinous' marble tongue unfurled within Hector's mouth like portent ice, the sign of a new age.

Interrupting their kiss, the living statue exclaimed, "But where are my manners? Forgive me. I have not asked you a single question. What is your name? I understand there is a great park outside this hall. Are you, perhaps, a shepherd there?"

Marcus rolled through the park, allowing his new form and instincts to drive him. Such freedom tasted of victory, as if his life before the infecting bite had been one of unwarranted restraint. Now he was free, naked strength pulsing against the night's chill, slave only to animal hunger. And he was ready to feast now.

He lurched toward the fleeing faun. He sensed his prey was about to stumble, and he leapt. He brought the terrified boy down with a crash, denting the already beleaguered grass with their soon-to-be copulating forms. Small, even for a faun, the boy cowered as Marcus bared diamond teeth, his lupine cock prodding tame abdomen, demanding entrance. The whimpering faun obeyed this insistent wand and scrambled onto his stomach, spreading his legs wide. Marcus bat at the faun's blonde haunches with a sharp paw. He mounted the boy with a

single, brutal thrust. The internal warmth of the boy wrapped his wolf-cock in pleasure; the saw of cicadas in the trees, the panting of far-off werewolves, the whisper of traffic just beyond the edge of the inimitable copse of the Ramble ... Marcus could even feel the vibration of night crawlers diligently churning cool soil far beneath his earth-gripping claws; every sensation flooded him. His cock, buried deep into the boy, hardened further. The captured faun, nearly unconscious from such a mixture of pleasure and pain, was startled to lucidity as the wolf atop him roughly turned him over on his back, gyrating roughly on the throbbing penis still planted within the hot berth of his ass.

Moaning with pleasure, one arm thrown across closed eyes to further shield him from the onslaught, the faun submitted himself to even deeper probing as Marcus forged further into the warm, tight grotto between wide-spread legs. He howled and reveled. Wolves in the distance acknowledged his newfound mastery in similar howls. A werewolf chorus arose. He was a member of the pack. The faun beneath him fainted as Marcus lanced his buttocks with hot semen. Far from spent, he leapt from the still form and bounded across the Ramble, searching for fresh prey. Occasional droplets of sperm fell from his still seething dick, clinging desperately to the bark of serious pines.

Just as Bill feared, Asterion boarded an uptown bus. Probably servicing some human, he thought. Indignation and anger welled up within him. Some old man with a penchant for Faery Folk, who treats him like a pet. An inexpensive pet, he thought, trotting blocks behind the bus at a leisurely pace, the long and weary vehicle apparently making all the local stops, opening its door every block or so with a mechanical sigh. "I wonder how much money the old guy gives him? Obviously not enough to buy shirts!" Bill immediately castigated himself for such a thought, unconsciously lashing his rump with his tail. It was wrong to judge him, or presuppose such matters. But here he was, following the boy.

Asterion had just moved to the city without a dime, and though he might enjoy Bill's company, even granting him real affection, he had to pay the rent. "Dear God, what if he really lives with the old scamp?" Bill shuddered just as the bus itself shuddered, shedding a few passengers, spilling out a fair amount of gray exhaust before picking up speed. He had to wonder if he was doing the right thing, following the lad, who had shown him nothing but deferential kindness, sincere warmth, and had proved the best damned lay he'd had inside a decade.

Bill stopped at the light to weigh his options, the bus idling, too, one block ahead. He was trailing a boy who had also been less-than-forthcoming, who never stayed the night. Should he count his blessings, turn tail, so-to-speak, and head home? No, the unanswered questions would gnaw at him, corrupting any future intimacy, though the very question of such intimacy would surely be answered if he were spotted. How could he ever explain such a rash action?

The light turned green, giving Bill the go ahead. He plowed after the bus, stopping short to allow a flock of impatient taxis to take the lead, least he overtake it and be seen. Luckily, he paused behind a traffic-stalled delivery van as ahead Asterion disembarked. With his head down, hands under his arms for warmth, Asterion marched across Fifty-Seventh Street toward the nocturnal darkness of Central Park. With renewed anger Bill pursued.

In the silence of the museum, Hector slowly caressed his marble lover. Antinous had led him to a cavernous room wherein the reconstructed Temple of Endymion proudly stood, resilient to the centuries, neatly secured by a slight moat of emerald calm, an atoll of copper coins beneath the water, a rusty fauna of verdigrised coral shimmering slightly. They lay on the cool floor in the center of the temple, wrapped in Napoleonic

graffiti, then older names and hexes in barely discernable Latin. Their skin reflected a milky phosphorescence beneath the streaming moonlight, as the massive gallery devoted to the temple was opened to the night, the entire western wall glass.

His strong-yet-pliable biceps gave way warmly beneath Antinous' firm grip, wherein the living statue was hard and smooth. Hector stroked his magical lover's back, running his fingers down to the wide curves of his rounded buttocks. This caused his formerly diminutive soldier, a pert, robust acorn punctuating a hairless navel, to grow and, pressed against Hector's waist, make for a rather formidable invader, much to his surprise. He knelt to kiss it. With this scepter against his lips, he could feel the stone further engorge and, though still cold, it emanated a mystical warmth. He wrapped his fingers around the prone cock and kissed Antinous with renewed vigor. He wondered what magic would be released once he parted his buttocks for this magic sword growing in his hand.

The living statue cupped his ass. Hector quivered at such strength and spread his legs slightly. Antinous gave a quick grin that held the same meaning across the centuries – he wanted in.

He positioned himself above Hector but the former faun surprised him by wiggling away, to again access to the living statue's cock with his mouth. Antinous arched his back and

sighed as Hector worked the length of the cool, rigid cock between his lips, generating more magic with his tongue than any spell Antinous would have encountered in the past. And Antinous was enthralled, slowly pumping the length of his penis between supple lips. Hector caught the sparkle of the statue's tight testicular orb, veins of purple lightning stirred just below the surface, accenting their hidden inner strength. Suddenly, Hector froze. I wonder what will happen when he cums? Antinous immediately sensed concern in his new lover.

"Do not worry, young one. I would never do anything to hurt you."

And they embraced. Boy and Statue. Boy becoming man, the living statue actually flush, white marble brushed pink from deep within, a human heart beating within a chest of stone. And for the first time in eons it quickened its pace.

Hector felt as if he were beached beside a river flowing over stone smoothed by the stream of centuries, the whispers of an internal brook close to divulging all of life's secrets. If only he could swim toward the subterranean source of this river, drinking from such resplendent water would banish all of his worries. And with their next kiss, he was further enchanted. He opened his legs and surrendered,

Warm stone parted him. His resistance melted as Antinous mounted him with the patience of a statue. Hector gasped; slowly Antinous placed his strength inside the boy. The magic that made him a statue kept his stone length from causing pain. Hector wrapped his legs around the statue to pull him further inside. Both moaned as Antinous rocked forward. He placed his cold, marble hands on Hector's chest. The boy thrashed beneath him, so much so that Antinous paused and shushed him with a kiss. It had been too long, eons since Antinous had reached orgasm. He could not control himself and Hector shook as hot semen filled him until it flowed out and pasted his thighs in sticky delight. Antinous groaned and shuddered and kneaded the boy's cock into orgasm. The statue collapsed. He turned to Hector and smiled.

"Now that was surely worth the wait."

Un-reigned by fury, Bill stormed the park. In full gallop he cut across traffic. Braking cabs swerved and drivers cursed as the mad centaur bolted heedlessly across the barren, weedy concrete round-about, through traffic, leaping in an instant the mossy, cobblestone fence. Seething with anger, his nostrils flared, gathering a cornucopia of scents: the sticky sweetness of spilled soda, sour urine, exhaust from the street, the musk of distant werewolves wafting through the air gave him pause.

Slowing to a trot, shocked at the loud drumming of his heart, he had second thoughts about following the boy into the Ramble, for werewolves hunger after centaurs in an entirely different manner; centuries ago, when unconfined by the diminishing magic of the world, the wolves roamed Mediaeval Europe in it's entirety, primarily feasting on centaurs. Bill shuddered at the thought, realizing that his scent, too, was now quite readily available to the wolves, and in no time soon, they would ascertain that his proximity was far closer than that of a straggling carriage. They would soon be upon him like the proverbial pack.

In his fit of jealousy, he had already made it halfway to Bow Bridge. He stood at an intersection where the emerald darkness deepened as the lampposts were strung farther and farther apart. As he turned to hasten his departure, he heard a slight rustle in the bushes not too far off the path. Fear gripped his heart. But so too did the scent of a familiar faun. Pain flooded his chest. However fleeting their relationship was to be, this pursuit was wrong. They should not meet like this. Still, to trot away and not confess his jealousy would be even more shameful. Bill ducked to avoid a low, heavy branch and made his way to where his young paramour lay in wait, no doubt thrilled at the prospect of an approaching virile werewolf. He imagined the shock as disappointment he would read on the

youth's face when he realized that he had been followed, his privacy invaded; their budding relationship would blossom into ridiculous travesty. It was Bill, however, who was surprised, stunned silent where he had expected to mutter apologies while watching something wonderful wilt to dust before his eyes.

Within the large, intertwined roots of a particularly massive oak, Asterion had smoothed out the earth and laid down a rather abused Indian rug rescued from some Upper West Side rubbish heap. A tattered knapsack hung neatly from the lowest branch, a tin of water was stowed snugly in the furthest reaches of the root's cleavage, along with a paper cup stuffed with basic toiletries. The startled faun was literally bowled over by Bill's intrusion. Falling on his back he looked about in desperation, as if he were contemplating escape. Much worse, Asterion looked totally ashamed. Bill's heart rocked with a newfound agony. Wherein he had pursued the boy out of jealousy, thinking the faun gaily headed for midnight mischief of the sort he disclaimed, in reality he was heading home, a home of his own making in Central Park.

Bill strove for the right words, to both apologize and immediately offer the comfort and security of his home. Asterion was speechless, too, wanting to explain that he hid his current situation from Bill so that the centaur would never think

they were together out of necessity on his part. He never meant to deceive him and indeed had never lied. But neither was afforded the opportunity to explain their situations as Asterion let loose a leaf-shaking sneeze, the faun's allergy suddenly activated.

Marcus railed at the moon; his lonely roar incited yet another chorus of werewolves thirsty for faun. As this luperwaul faded, the blue tips of the taller trees clashed lightly in the wind. From his rocky perch, he sniffed a lone faun hovering on the outskirts of the Ramble – his tiny heartbeat rang like a distant church bell in the hollow of his long, furry ears. He slid from his rock and turned quietly through the trees toward the unsuspecting faun. Sniffing the air, he did not detect the scent of any other werewolf moving in the same direction. Marcus quickened his pace.

Striding confidently over Bow Bridge, Marcus was certain he was the only werewolf bold enough to move outside the Ramble, this segment of the park was now entirely his domain; the faun who currently enraptured his senses had nestled down not too far ahead. He thought that if this boy didn't give too much chase, he might have a chance at a third faun before dawn, and a pang of agreement issued from the ruby cock rising from between his haunches.

Hunger led him in a westerly direction, though now he had resumed a more stealthy position on all fours, slicing through the brush silently with his black snout, to better take his prey by surprise. As he filtered the various scents wafting through the night air to keep a fix on the faun, Marcus suddenly reeled, assaulted by a startling aroma, the rosy explosion enriching his nostrils … familiar meat. Impossible. Suicidal. A centaur had entered Central Park at night. The suppressed human portion of his mind surfaced with surprise to report that this was an unheard-of transgression and an impossible risk. This lone human voice was quickly shredded as the werewolf Marcus, no longer stunned, quickly asserted himself, for the moon was full, his hunger strong, and the appetite for centaur far surpassed that of faun. Frozen in his tracks, lower to the ground, he assayed the landscape, allowing his senses to widen until his perception of the park stretched beyond his immediate desire: no other wolf had yet caught the centaur's scent and exited the Ramble, all were too caught up in the prey before them to perceive the treasure tramping around just outside their erotic boundaries.

Marcus had good reason to be so cautious toward both his newfound prey and the other wolves. A treat as rare as this was worth fighting for. For fauns seek out werewolves, and enjoy their brutal company. They know that past the chase,

beyond the fear, they will survive to entreat with werewolves yet again. Centaurs are not so lucky. Saliva darkened the soil beneath his carnivorous crotch. With a renewed determination, he moved closer to where the centaur seemed to have been waylaid.

Familiar meat. Sure, he knew the scent. Now he craved the taste.

Bill placed one finger to his lips, begging silence from the teary faun. With the other hand he motioned that the boy should pack his things quickly. Both sensed a werewolf was about. As Asterion gathered his bedding into the tattered maw of his knapsack, a quiet menace emanated from within the dark folds of tree and bush.

Lowering his hind quarters, Bill waved the boy up on his back, hoping to flee before the waiting carnivore decided to attack. Too late: the werewolf Marcus tore out of the brush, launching himself at the centaur, not realizing that the man-horse's position of a pro-offered ride made him a natural spring. And so Bill simultaneously reared, newly forged strength pulsing through muscles well-exercised from his jealously-fueled romp. Buoyed by a decade of weariness, his years of tedious discrimination had fermented into a coil of bile; with

this coursing black adrenaline he instinctively, willfully lashed out. Both of his hooves met Marcus' furry jaw with a wet crack.

Fang bent and blood fanned out. Asterion cried, scrambling backwards into the roots of the oak. In full fury, Bill trampled the stunned werewolf, surprised at the thickness of the form beneath his hooves. Bones snapped beneath his weight.

It was over before the leaves had settled.

The centaur stood above the broken beast, the wolf's red tongue hung limp, caked with dirt, nostrils bubbling with blood. Panting, Bill's chest heaved. His hands shook. He took a deep breath to regain his composure. Turning, he extended a sweaty hand to Asterion, again bending his hind legs to offer the faun a ride. Asterion emerged from the roots shaken, but with his knapsack full, ready for departure. He climbed upon Bill's back and hid his face between his shoulder blades, reaching around to grasp his sweaty, firm chest.

Chapter 12. Temples at Dawn

How small a fraction of all the measureless infinity of time is allotted to each of us; an instant, and it vanishes into eternity. How puny, too, is your portion of all the world's substance; how insignificant your share of all the world's soul; on how minute a speck of the whole earth do you creep. As you ponder these things, make up your mind that nothing is of any import save to do what your own nature directs, and to bear what the world's Nature sends you.

– Marcus Aurelius

Prelude to dawn: the muffled twitter of birds from just outside the museum windows gently woke the lovers. The twisting corolla of the rising sun seeped into the glass with a sliding rainbow of fresh color. Barrett stirred. Up on one elbow,

he admired the supine perfection of Antinous. He marveled at the breathing statue. Unasked questions clung to his mind like a sturdy, intractable fog. Where do we go from here? How do we continue? As Hector imagined a life lived beneath a cramped dining room table, of stolen scraps of food and midnight folly, his statue lover opened his marble eyes and rose.

"Come. The museum will open soon."

Before he could ask any questions, Antinous firmly grasped Hector's hand and whisked him from the temple's portico and into the winding Egyptian halls. He led him to a dim, obscure room, the lights low to protect ancient papyrus pressed to the wall by a sheet of thick, dusty glass. Opposite the papyrus stood youthful male caryatids, servile stone, hands flat above their heads, forever hoisting a great weight long ago removed by the vagaries of time. Hector tried to discern their faces. Worn smooth by the centuries, they seemed blissful, unconcerned. Antinous studiously positioned Hector among the caryatids, molding his shoulders and raising his arms in a perfect caricature of the statues. They froze at the sound of guards passing through the next room.

As Hector was about to express bemused doubt that he could maintain this position for an entire day, that and the

room's dimness surely wasn't enough to disguise his humanity, Asterion placed both hands on his cheeks and kissed him with a deep, singular longing. A heaviness instantly surrounded him. His raised arms seemed to thicken, his feet felt rooted to the floor. A thick river of sleep engulfed the room. The silt of an undefined fear rose to cloak his vision in an opaque darkness. Hector wanted to call out but could not find his voice. He fought against this river but found himself frustratingly immobile. He could barely glance down; a steady tide of earthy rust ran up his legs, clasping his genitalia, reaching toward his torso. Hector was turning to stone.

Vision grayed further toward blackness. Antinous was a shadow; the wall of yellowed papyrus read a desert expanse, a new playground for the dreams galloping majestically toward him, leading the rising tide of sleep. Resolve weakening, he heard Antinous speak. His voice sounded as if it were carried from afar on a dry wind.

"Do not be afraid. We will be together soon."

The shadow of his lover receded. Distantly he heard, "I love you."

An echo on the wind, he eased into slumber. Permanent or fleeting, Hector did not care.

Back at his apartment, Bill paced the hoof-scuffed floor while Asterion splashed around in the bath. Though the near full gallop home had exhausted his supply of adrenalin, his cheeks were seared red, his mind racing. The way the boy clung to his neck, flush on his back as he steered through traffic, was somehow prescient, marking an untried but preferred sense of reliance. Bill felt he had done more than defend a lover, he had invited consequence. His heart was a fist of marble, a well-wrought copy veined and purple – exact in every detail excepting the crushing weight. Often he felt as if he had reached a point in his life where his past was so much more available than the future. It gave precedent to his ruminations. The present was a single wisp of a tome between uneven, portentous bookends. But what if Asterion was the sole poem in that little book? To be read aloud everyday and never quite understood; the best of poems are so faceted. Like this boy.

He heard water draining from the tub. Looking about the singular room, he found himself. His was not a life of bookends but one of music stands. Inviting, always open.

Asterion stepped from the bathroom. A damp, worn towel hung from his clasped hands, swaying between spindly, goatish legs. Clean hooves shone obsidian; bright droplets of water hung like diamonds from his matted, furry thighs. Bill felt

a pang of longing in his penis and quickly retrained his thoughts to the situation at hand. "Asterion…" But before he could continue the faun interrupted.

"Bill, I'm sorry."

"You have nothing to apologize for."

"I put you in danger! A centaur in Central Park at night – it's, it was suicide."

Bill bent his forelegs until he was eye-level with the boy. Hands on his shoulders, "If I had known your situation, I would have demanded you stay with me. That was pure foolishness."

His sure and steady gaze, meant to convey assurance, elicited fresh tears from the faun. Asterion had sobbed for blocks during their journey uptown; the mane at the small of the centaur's back was still damp from his tears.

"Asterion, don't cry. I love you and want to care for you."

And he did. The words flew out of his mouth before he had time to sift them through mere analysis. Care. He had had many lovers in the past, had sought fauns throughout the city

and, before that, men. Always though, he stood apart from his partners. He enjoyed their company, lusting for some, loving, really loving, just a few. But this was a new emotion, a field vaster than his previous romps had allowed, a terrain wondrous and worth exploring, though not without difficulty. It would require time and patience to navigate.

"I love …I … I … love you, too, Bill. That's why I didn't ever stay the night. I didn't want you to think I was using you, that I needed a place to stay as much as I needed you." He hid his face in his hands and broke away from the centaur's grip.

Bill reached out again and pulled him into his chest. The boy heaved. Bill kissed the small crown of Asterion's skull that shone through the reedy part of his thick, wet, strawberry locks. Asterion looked up. Bill pressed his lips to the boy's trembling mouth.

It was the best kiss of his life.

Calmly, the centaur pulled back. He remembered past lovers, some mere flirtations, others that scorched his heart, the few he had too readily pressed for something more permanent, possibly sabotaging what would have occurred if he had been willing to allow the relationship to bloom outside the tight

hothouse of immediate passion. And then there was the army of the dismissed, forever standing at attention, a battalion ever ready to lay siege to his subconscious. When he was at his "peak," so-to-speak, he had left boys crying at one bar while he absconded to the next nightclub, sure that a new and exhilarating erotic distraction would always be there for the taking. To invite Asterion to live with him now, no matter how sincere, meant turning his apartment into a safety deposit box, vouchsafing their relationship. It would never grow in value under such conditions. No, the faun would have to come in later, having established more than just his desire to be with the centaur. Asterion had to develop and grow on his own before either of them would earn the ability to thrive together.

Reaffirming his grip on the young faun, Bill steadied himself.

"I love you. I want you to stay with me until we can find you the right apartment. We will do this the right way." He brought his forehead closer, touching their brows together. "But you will always have a place in my heart."

Rudy had worked mornings with the Parks Department for a few years now. The youngest of the morning crew, he liked the park empty. At dawn the park seemed settled, a private world, distinct from the tourist and jogger-filled realm it would

179

become in a few hours. Most mornings, the core of every tunnel retained the previous night's shadows; outcroppings of rock glistened with dew, everything somewhat primordial, as if not yet available for human occupancy. And the discoveries he made. Every week brought some new mystery. Typical finds: shredded underwear and liquor bottles, drained save a cotillion of inebriated spiders bunched at the bottom, reveling in the remaining sluice of ambrosia. The most memorable sight yet, sundry shoes arranged in a ghostly parade around Bethesda Fountain. The empty, battered husks marched down the steps into the placid, murky waters of the tranquil pond. A waltz of empty suicides – a harrowing sight, truly the most memorable, until now, that is.

Pushing thick, oily hair out of his eyes, he crouched by the damaged body of the wolf and smoked the first joint of the morning. Afraid to get too close, he had heard or read somewhere that injured animals were prone to lash out at their saviors. However, Rudy soon realized the poor beast was unconscious, and even then in no shape to take a bite out of anybody. Probably it had been hit by a car. Cabs often cross the park at night; a few of the main traverses remain open at all hours. But he had found the wolf in a relatively wooded area. Possibly the poor creature dragged itself this far after being hit. But this is no dog. It's too big.

Obviously, a wolf had escaped the Central Park Zoo.

Ragged breath was barely discernable through blood-caked fur. He thought about radioing Animal Control but that would require filling out a police report as well. Better to just take the wolf back himself. They must have a veterinarian on staff. He inhaled deeply and screwed the remnants of his joint into the ground.

Rudy adroitly backed his all-terrain vehicle up to the wolf and unloaded the cargo of rakes and empty trash bins. The hard part was lifting the animal. He made a quick sled from an empty trash-bag and pulled him close to the trailer; the creature was heavier than it looked. Loading him was easy though; the trailer's rear door acted as an automated forklift – this was how they transported anything too hefty to carry through the park.

As he sped toward the zoo, Rudy peered over his shoulder to check on the animal. I must be high, a wolf in Central Park? The beast's breathing seemed stronger, more regular. Maybe it would be alright after all.

Marcus convalesced well past noon.

Doctor Van Cortlandt, the Central Park veterinarian, was not perplexed by the sudden appearance of a wolf. While

ushering him out the door, he was quick to scold the Parks Department employee that the wounded animal was obviously a large dog. Pretending to be insulted, he declared that it was impossible for a wolf to have escaped. But the young doctor who tended the multitude of creatures housed at the rather decrepit institution did so with an ulterior motive; the feathers and fur of such a variety of species were invaluable to a warlock of his ilk. Not that his care of the animals was secondary. No, his concern for the zoo's residents was as sincere as his specific needs: a licorice menagerie of crow served as aerial eyes, locating herbs important to his potions throughout the park. Slender snakes willingly forsook their scales, faded owls eventually parted with their feathers, all to serve the infamous Upper East Side Coven of Warlocks.

As their youngest member, Van Cortlandt was tasked with gathering ingredients necessary for their spells. Thus the werewolf now imprisoned in the straw-filled cage along with several very curious, very real wolves was invaluable. Werewolf semen is an element crucial to several complex incantations, its extraction typically more than an exacting affair, making a sleeping werewolf a real find.

The young warlock swiftly pulled back his long, blondish-white hair into a ponytail, just enough to still conceal

sharp, elfin ears. He removed his lab coat, soiled with dark smears of werewolf blood. He had bandaged and tranquilized the rapidly healing animal, somewhat surprised to discover wounds caused by the hooves of a powerful horse. Sharp black eyebrows arching, the warlock was curious but nonplussed; he knew that nothing but silver was fatal to a werewolf. But that's not to say that all action is without consequence. A lesser-known fact of Faery Folk lore is that a werewolf caught past dawn in wolf-form remains a full, four-legged animal for the length of that day. And, if imprisoned, cannot regain human form so long as bars exist between it and an apathetic moon.

Regarding the recovering wolf, he noted that it was smaller in stature than the animal wolves that shared his prison. And they were all male. He could tell from their anxious pacing, constantly stooping to sniff at the slumbering werewolf's exposed rear, that tonight they would fight among themselves for the right to dominate this newest addition to their brethren. The winner would claim the newcomer as his mate. But such rivalries only last so long. Likely the leader of the pack will lose interest. Only then will they all share in the spoils. The young warlock smiled and drew his long, effeminate fingers to the pale point of his chin, thinking he would stay past the zoo's closing just to witness the impending orgy. He imagined the werewolf's surprise and frustration, roughly taken from behind by his

merciless, more-feral cousins, unable to do anything other than bay at a starless sky devoid of any hope, silently pleading for release with all-too-human eyes. Such a promising exhibition warranted including the other members of the coven. Crows were called from the nearby trees and invitations to the celebration were sent out, post-hast.

Rent was due. The sadness pervading the apartment made pending payment a bitter chore. And their gorgon landlady did not suffer capricious fauns; it was long rumored that those overly late on their rent now adorned numerous parks. Stone fauns frozen in mid-frolic with birdbaths balanced atop rocky heads.

Barrett tossed the gold cufflinks in his closed fist as if they were luckless dice. Chelsea pawnshops know something of the Banquet and toward the end of the month will seriously underpay any Faery Folk who come selling valuable trinkets. He had weathered the long walk across town, then north, toward the Upper East Side, hoping the neighborhood proprietors there would be less inclined to take advantage of poor, put-upon fauns. He was disappointed to find that, though the businesses were obviously open, the doors were locked; you had to be buzzed in. Shopkeepers all kept their heads down, or further

engaged customers, ignoring his presence. Dejected, he walked toward the water.

At the foot of the Fifty-ninth Street Bridge's sooty ascendancy, like a giant, traffic-clogged stairway to Olympus, Barrett noticed the faint smell of troll wafting among the car exhaust and sea-scents from the nearby brackish river. He spied a small antique shop, its door propped open to receive the late summer breeze. Well, I've come this far. I should try one more. Shoulders slumped he slinked across the street and peered into the shop. Small, inviting, he could tell instantly that this shop specialized in objects relating to Faery Folk lore. And as such, the abundant collection gave off a collective, calming radiance, making this less a place of commerce and more half-temple, a certain sanctuary.

Close to the inviting entrance the noise of traffic ceased. Enveloped in near silence, Barrett thought he could perceive the far-off sounds of the Ramble at twilight, whispering trees, the childish chanting of midnight fountains. Sheepish, he stood on the cusp of the entryway; Barrett was weary of yet another surly merchant. In the window, a dusty caduceus was placed reverently among an array of faint gold leaf laurels, surrounded by miniature busts of deities known and unknown. An assortment of pottery shards, seemingly displayed at random,

appeared to secretly spell something in a language familiar but forgotten.

The proprietor caught Barrett's eye and gave him a warm, welcoming smile. The cufflinks in his palm suddenly felt light, like airy game pieces particular to this room of magical antiquities. His first thought was to just turn around and leave immediately, walk briskly to the river and throw the cufflinks into the water. Then, lurching past paranoia, he wondered, what if their magic was strong? What if twin golden Golems emerged from the murky waters to come after me?

"Don't worry, little faun. Those cufflinks are magical, yes, but their real value is that they are simply pure gold."

Barrett was startled; one hoof in the door, he wanted to flee the potential powers of this obvious warlock, but something stayed him.

"I'm no warlock, little faun. And I cannot see your thoughts. The cufflinks possess a simple charm, to always return to their owner."

And with that the proprietor smiled a familiar smile. Tall, his dark skin looked warmer in the well-lit store than in the high midnight tower of the Banquet. His broad shoulders

casually filled his lightly starched, open-collared shit; his proud skull shone, luminous, as if a conduit for the enchanted items in the surrounding cases and cabinets. Even in human form, Barrett recognized his Dark Wolf. Full, confident lips spread to reveal gleaming, perfect teeth. The faun blushed as the wolf-now-human caught him furtively eying the ample coil hanging beneath his silver belt buckle. Its smooth portrait of a menacing Medusa brought him back to reality.

"I should return these to you."

He held out his hand and uncurled his fingers. The gold cufflinks were fogged – cloudy from the heat of his nervous fist.

"No, they were a present. I am, however, prepared to buy them back. I know their exact worth. And that I will pay you, if you will grant me one wish."

Barrett gulped. Flushed, whether from being in the presence of such a desirable man or from the powers of the charmed gold still heavy in his hand, he shifted on his hooves. Swallowing, he remained quiet, to see what else the Dark Wolf required of him.

"Have no fear, my little faun. The Banquet can be brutal. All I'm asking for is dinner."

At that they both laughed. Any untoward tension thus banished, Barrett stepped forward to the counter. The Dark Wolf opened the antique cash register. The ornate brass machine sounded a quaint, intimate alarm – announcing more than a mere monetary transaction.

Dusk twinkled and flared, ignited by the kiss of a living god. Hector felt air returning to unused lungs, his torso heavy and static, like a big machine rusting in a forgotten field. He did not gulp for air; it eased into him like a breeze. Vision slowly returned. He felt peaceful, rested and rightly noble, as a marble statue must. Giggling at such a spurious thought, he wavered. Antinous caught him and whispered for him to be quiet, that he must not alert the museum guards.

"I'm sorry if I took you by surprise. There was not much time. You were naked and I was far from my pedestal ..." Hector realized the living statue was struggling for the right words in a language overheard and underused.

"I understand," he quickly interrupted. "It was just so sudden, but I ... I think I dreamed the impossible. It's like I ... I found this other temple. Or another museum. I'm ... I'm not sure."

Hector blinked, trying to summon the fading memory of long halls and vast cathedrals; his returning flesh flushed out salty tears, new saliva rolled in his mouth.

Antinous spoke softly, his timbre proud. "I knew you would be fine. The world inside can be a dark, barren landscape. Or a city of light. It took me years beneath that river to wander from the scarred fields of my grief to the more wondrous parts of my mind. Something told me it wouldn't take you quite so long."

He took the former faun by the hand. They wound their way through various galleries. This time Antinous asked many questions, about both his life and the outside world. As they walked the living statue would stop before certain works of art and discuss their meaning, then turn the conversation back to Hector's barely recalled dream world. One such work reminded the former consort of a hunting trip in Egypt. Another would incite questions about the city outside. Hector had almost forgotten the park, the city! There were so many adventures awaiting him here, within the confines of the museum; it was easy to forget the trials of the Faery world.

Foot steps. Guards were approaching. They had wandered far from their statuary brethren, up some inviting stairs through galleries of large modern paintings mute and

shallow minus the overhead lights and chirping crowds. Having scanned the room for exits, Hector looked nervously toward his lover. Antinous smiled knowingly and stepped back against the wall; he froze beside a vast, nonsensical landscape of grays, blues and blacks. Fear filled the former faun, the approaching guards were close. And he understood. Assuming a similar position opposite Antinous, on the other side of the painting, as if they were part of some installation, Hector closed his eyes in concentration.

He now had this power.

But how to describe it? For lack of a better word, Hector immediately felt constipated. No, that wasn't it. He closed his now suddenly-marble eyelids and cast his vision inward. The tall cathedral of his mind opened to inspection as never before. An endless dome rose above him symmetrically, billowing with gothic detail. Ornate balustrades dripped down the walls. Everywhere fountains sang silently of spring. He touched the supporting pedestal of one of the balustrades, mimesis struck; here was the foundation of a single thought he had had as a child, the kernel of an idea, one worthy of retention, from which support for an entire host of ideas grew, forming temples on the other side of the supporting wall. Craving entry, he began to

wonder which among the myriad of fine corridors led inside when his name echoed throughout the cathedral.

"Hector, Hector ..."

Awake, he instantly assumed human form. Blinking, the living statue stood before him, smiling proudly.

"That … that was wonderful."

"You are beautiful. And honest, your temples are unbroken. And worth exploring." Antinous' grin grew foxish. Forehead to forehead he whispered closely, "Now won't you let me inside?"

They slid to the floor. As Hector steadied himself for this new embrace, he realized that, as the heart has chambers, the mind has churches and vaults, everything was theirs to explore. Forever. With each kiss they shone like two temples at dawn, lit from an internal sun, destined to outshine the external city far from their sacred ground.

They will continue to join in the dark. They will meet like this when the museum is long forgotten, boarded up; they will kiss as the park slowly pushes into the galleries, as impertinent roots sift the marble floor and tree limbs push through the roof. Wars flash across the sky like so much

lightning. They will hold hands as the ocean casually ascends. And when the waters withdraw, and they stand among faceless statues stroked by fresh dunes, they will build something new.

Chapter 13. Autumn Heralds

And the sight of it all

Makes me sad and ill.

That's when I want

Some weird sin

– Iggy Pop

Christopher felt lost. Barrett had not returned from his errand – that, coupled with Hector's sudden departure, made the apartment seem huge and barren; he felt as if he were trespassing in his own home. Too much had happened of late for him to have no one to counsel and console him, to explain things. Overwhelmed, he thought to find comfort, at least physical comfort, in the Ramble, and had decided to walk

uptown, meandering over to Broadway, nearly aimless, eventually though, he would run into the park. Yet as the sun set, the breeze stiffened. He noticed young couples holding each other closely. The elderly were already equipped with trusty sweaters. The first touch of autumn was in the air. He could only imagine the chill that was taking hold in the Ramble. The thought of such frolic lost its appeal.

He had heard about the park in winter. Come fall, the trees thin, and when they are finally bare, the werewolves retire. Fauns nestle down in their apartments, hibernating, roused now and again by more rambunctious roommates to forage for food – daring each other to run out into the snow, to plop down and flap their arms and legs, making snow harpies in the street. Will he have that, absenting Hector? And what of Barrett? He knew the rumors of their gorgon landlady ... Christopher shivered, whether from the rising wind or the numerous, ever-branching thoughts scratching at the unknown, until lost in an interior thicket of clawing possibilities, he wavered. Confused, dejected, he changed direction near Times Square.

The lights and tall buildings around him seemed dissonant, repellant even. The Ramble might have held a dissipating interest, but he knew of another place where

passions are not hostage to the seasons, somewhere deep and internal. He increased his pace with a renewed vigor.

The evening blossomed as Barrett and Renaud walked across town. Couples spilled out of restaurants, gleefully clinging to one another, exuberant with the sudden change in weather. They had dined at a discrete little café near Bryant Park. In the candlelit intimacy his werewolf suitor properly introduced himself, Renaud. The youngest of the Werewolves of Wall Street, he eschewed the wantonness of the Ramble, but was only half-committed to the wild austerity of the Banquet. As yet, he was not completely at home with his wealthier werewolf compatriots; he was valuable to them not as an equal but as a procurer for the enchanted items necessary to accentuate their lofty stations. Barrett listened closely, for more than a tale was being told; within the contours of his past, he felt the Dark Wolf was issuing an invitation for the future. They held hands under the table during dessert and coffee and continued holding hands on the way home.

Back at the apartment, the faun felt something was amiss. Christopher should be here, Barrett thought. Stalling, flitting around the room, straining for conversation, finally worried that Renaud would become uncomfortable just waiting without reason, he explained his dilemma. Of course Renaud

understood the situation; having seen the cadre of roommates at the last Banquet, it was apparent that as much as one faun was on the cusp of the change, the other was as much the neophyte. And the change had now forced his roommate out; the boy had lost a guardian, his first friend. Barrett confessed that he felt he should have been there to fill his hooves. But he had put financial concerns above all else, and worse, dallied over the possibility of an affair. With this last comment, chin to chest, he looked up at his werewolf paramour, expecting to be scolded outright. But Renaud spoke in a soothing tone.

"I know the gorgons that run many of these apartment buildings, little one. You did the right thing. Better you procure rent than end up in some Park Slope garden, balancing a birdbath on your head for all eternity. Now where would that leave your friend? Likely he's at your favorite pub, or skipping through the Ramble."

He reached out with both hands and with his thumbs smoothed the full locks curling atop his lover's head. But Barrett was unsure. There was the latent scent of despair about the room, that blind cousin to desperation. Even in human form, Renaud, too, could decipher the smell from among the innumerable stuffy odors permeating the fauns' flat. They looked at each other. If Christopher entered Pluto's Basement

without paying, a single kiss there could spell his doom. They paused to absorb the full meaning of their collective dread then raced down the stairs and out into the night.

Rudy cautiously entered the park at night. He had approached from the Upper East Side, weaving between mansions and embassies, their forlorn and majestic flags hung over his head like a flock of spectral vultures. The mystery of the wounded dog ate him all day: the animal couldn't be feral. And any New Amsterdam dog-owner would have searched the park frantically, putting up posters all over town. When he brought the animal in, the barely concealed delight in the veterinarian's eye gleamed like a purloined diamond secreted a purse of white velvet. The man's haughtiness repulsed him, yet he could not stop thinking of him. After finishing his shift he had several beers at a pub near the subway. As his co-workers drifted home, he remained at the bar with his unclear thoughts. He hadn't planned to enter the park; he and his colleagues had long snickered about the rumored midnight rendezvous among men, the danger of the Ramble after dark, but after so many beers and much hazy rumination, he had to piss.

His meanderings had led him close to the zoo. Its gothic entrance, so dramatic and historical during the day, now loomed in the shadows like a giant's gaping mouth, toothless yet greedy

and full of foreboding. Rudy shivered and searched for a suitable tree. Shadows moved. He unzipped his jeans and took out his cock. It looked timid in the moonlight. Urine started and stopped in nervous spurts as he looked over his shoulder. Suddenly sober, he felt annoyed at how withdrawn and tiny his dick was in his hand, as if it embodied the embarrassing fear that dissipated his well-earned buzz. He tugged at it angrily, demanding it harden. Like a dog on a leash, his cock responded to his rough handling and rose slowly, wavering as droplets of urine clung to his hairy testicles like fresh dew. He was surprised by his own brazenness. A sexual energy crackled around him. He felt his intoxication restored; a barely detectable scent wafted from the zoo, other-worldly yet with a familiar musk. This was different from the buzz he got from beer and poorly-rolled joints; he pulled his shirt out and unbuttoned it. He wanted to be naked. The breeze combed his pubic hair like invisible fingers; his cock further engorged at this magical sensation. Shadows no longer seemed threatening but inviting. He rushed to push off his pants and pulled off his shirt. The closeness of the street and buildings were an affront to his desires; he wanted darkness and the touch of another. He heard a canine cry from the zoo and thought of the wounded animal from this morning. "Am I not now its natural protector?" An irrational thought, yet he was naked in a world of alluring

shadows, a nighttime world he had previously derided and never understood. Now he stood as an initiate. Rudy gripped the hair that covered his chest and pulled. He breathed deeply. There it was again, stronger: light incense masking the smell of sweat and something robust, animal. It demanded to be petted, wrestled to the ground and controlled. Novice or master, Rudy was willing to join. He walked toward the entrance, ready to be swallowed fully by the forces within.

The young warlock was pleased. Many of the coven's most senior members had immediately convened after receiving the word of his discovery. Word carried by crow. Not only are they the eyes of the East Side Warlocks, but the birds also served as a feathered telegraph system, bringing word of deed or simple warlock-gossip to the windowsills of many a townhouse. More warlocks materialized, stepping out of shadows or transforming from regal owls as they landed among others gathering in the zoo's central and rather cramped faux-medieval piazza, which was encircled by cages, some empty, one packed with wolves.

Van Cortlandt did not bother to lay out any delicacies for his guests but served a simple wine. Among the senior warlocks, he did not want to be known as one who curried favor, just one who got results. So many of his peers played

politics; he noticed that among the oldest and wisest there was only one commonality – spell-craft. Survival in an enchanted world depended more on ability then manners and alliances. Allies die. But to know the spells of transformation and to have the precious, necessary ingredients on hand, that was how a warlock prospers and survives centuries at a time. And with this observation, he chose to serve his elders in a more valuable capacity. By gathering the herbs and necessary accoutrements for their spells, he was able to glean knowledge often of little interest to his more social peers. Of the younger warlocks who travel in owl-form, only he knew the spell to become a trail of smoke. And though he kept this ability a secret from the coven, they would have not been jealous. They would think him foolish to bypass the showy, formal shape of an owl. But they were not thinking like the older warlocks. Bullets and arrows pass through smoke and little else. The war with the West Side Coven may be in one of its long phases of inactive suspicion, but truces are made to be broken. Barely one hundred years old, Van Cortlandt was considered scarcely an adolescent by the coven, but he craved the knowledge of the ages.

An older warlock approached, his black velvet cloak clung to him like the wings of a thirsty bat. He reached out and stroked Van Cortlandt's hair.

"This is a fine discovery. I must say the elders of the coven are impressed."

Van Cortlandt nodded in sincere appreciation. Praise from a senior warlock is rare indeed.

"And we recognize this as the result of hard work, not chance." His hand remained on Van Cortlandt's cheek, firm and strong. Their eyes locked, and a mystical moment arose. An erotic exchange of physical possibilities blossomed in their minds as they shared thoughts of hot bodies intertwined, unrivaled lust and the cry of wolves.

The elder warlock blinked, and contact was broken. Van Cortlandt felt the loss. All that he had worked so hard for could be gone in an instant. The warlock sensed the youth's bewilderment and cupped the young man's chin. Long fingers with polished nails scratched playfully at the wisp of stubble. Van Cortlandt felt soothed. His elder left to mingle with the arriving coven. In the cage, animals paced, aroused and enchanted. Each arriving warlock added his power to the charms that both protected their brethren's gathering and cast a spell over the wolves. No one outside would suspect or even hear anything unusual. Humans would find themselves naturally disinclined to approach. However, anyone that might feel the enchantments pull would surrender to the power of the coven.

Warlocks are always on the lookout for servants or new familiars.

As the coven gathered, Van Cortlandt readied the proceedings. He lit black candles made from the dust of dragon bones. The powerful incense of their flame added a demonic undertone to the night's air. Warlocks leant him their power with whispered incantations. A canopy of smoke formed over the group. Inky shadows between the stone flooring pulsed and bubbled. Goblins began to emerge.

The goblins that lived in the dark caves beneath Central Park kept to themselves and rarely trafficked with other Faery Folk. They forged their gold solely to covet and traded only when coerced. As subways and waterworks threatened their habitat, an alliance with the East Side Coven was forced. So dedicated to their art and ignorant of the Machiavellian machinations, warlocks were known for, they never suspected just how much of the human encroachment was manipulated by the warlocks to encourage just such a partnership. They provided gold items to be charmed by the warlocks, and in turn, no tunnels were dug. Their caves seemingly protected when in fact the city itself had a ban on subways crossing beneath the park.

Black living oil streamed from between the cracks of the stone flooring and quickly flowed into small ebony humanoid forms. The hairless goblins were so dark, their skin so shiny, it was hard to discern facial features. Their muscular frames glowed in the candlelight. They stretched and yawned as they solidified. Long, pointed ears stirred the smoke that had summoned them. They cracked their knuckles, adding a rude percussion to the warlock's chanting and softly snapping fingers. The magic of the coven was always hypnotic to them. They arose aroused. Their tiny, needle-like cocks swung like miniature scimitars before their plump bellies. Each goblin sought a warlock to adhere to; and they accordingly opened their robes to accept the shadowy ministrations of groping black claws and enthusiastic mouths. Younger mages drew protectively closer to their older benefactors, chanting in their ears while stroking their own crotches. Van Cortlandt opened the cage and let the wolves out.

The wolf Marcus was shocked by the smoky proceedings. He howled plaintively and choked on the mystical, acrid smoke. The other wolves eyed him with a vigorous lust that filled him with fear while his red dog dick betrayed him. It slid from its furry sheath to hang between his hindquarters like an incandescent beacon. Thick electrical enchantment guided the animals to their task. They circled one another, growling,

baring their teeth. Marcus felt a rough muzzle lift his tail. A wolf tongue lapped at his rear. Sharp teeth grated his flanks. He whimpered, but his disloyal cock quivered and lengthened. The wolf circle quickened their pace.

Van Cortlandt withdrew to the center table, a stone slab covered with his instruments and candles. The other warlocks were fully engrossed with the demonic circus; many had parted their cloaks and dropped their trousers to allow goblins to feed at their cocks. A few playfully stirred their fingers in a goblin's black ass while watching the wolves. Goblins greedily lapped at the rigid cocks cracking their ebony lips. Young warlocks stripped and stood in provocative poses to catch the eyes of their elders. Magnificent, goblin-wrought white gold bracelets slid down thin wrists as they reached for the night sky. Senior warlocks gave the chosen a commanding stare. The younger members of the coven slid across the cold stone floor and lowered themselves. They joined a fleet of goblins in supplication.

Rudy watched the proceedings from behind an empty cage. Though shocked, nothing could break the enchantment that urged him forward. It took all his strength to keep from joining in. "Will I be welcome? Will those black things tear me apart?" He marveled at the sexual demons writhing before the

warlocks. And he sensed that the men gathered there were magical, the cause of the enchantment. Pointed ears broke long flaxen, often white, hair. They were all similarly slender and tall. Rudy marveled at the extraordinary length of bejeweled fingers and thought of the handsome veterinarian he had delivered the injured animal to. He's here, I feel his presence. And Rudy knew with an unfamiliar certainty that he was here to serve, and he knew whom to approach. For the first time in his life, the smoke in his mind cleared. Internal stars sparkled with new clarity. He separated himself from the pillar and calmly walked among warlock and goblin, seeking his new master.

Van Cortlandt casually pushed away an eager goblin with his foot. Heat emanated from the gyrating couple pressed up against him. He unbuttoned his shirt and sought some air. Absentmindedly fingering the slight hair knitted across his chest, he walked toward the edge of the crowd. A wolf howled. Then another. Van Cortlandt smirked and thought that the night was a success, nothing could go wrong. And then he spied a naked human. He nearly spat a deadly hex in his direction but hesitated. He recognized him. It was that dumb Parks employee who had delivered the werewolf to him. Van Cortlandt swallowed the poisonous magic coiled on his tongue. The parks employee had struck him as just another wayward human, without drive or purpose. But naked, he seemed sure of himself,

and his body was wonderful, naturally sculpted by labor to be of considerable use to an up-and-coming warlock. Rudy stepped forward. Van Cortlandt struggled to reign in his surprise and happiness and instead shot the human a cool, appraising look. Rudy dropped to one knee and bowed his head. He placed steady, strong hands on Van Cortlandt's sleek leather boots. The warlock approved of the strong shoulders spread before him.

"Stand."

Rudy rose. Eye to eye, they both reached for each other.

"If you are to serve me, to give me your life in its entirety, then I must first serve you."

The warlock cocked his head and narrowed his eyes, awaiting the human's answer. Rudy breathed deeply the scent of magic and mystery. His decision to enter the park at night was no drunken accident. He thought back. Nor was it just chance that he found a job here. To serve this warlock would deepen his knowledge of the earth he tilled and policed during the day. Now he was offered a night-shift; he would be allowed to lift the gossamer curtain that existed between two worlds that occupied the same space. A contrarily cherubic goblin absently wrapped a warm claw around his ankle while servicing a nearby warlock. Rudy silently accepted the invitation.

Van Cortlandt placed his hands on Rudy's strong chest and felt the honesty and power within. He lingered there for a moment, leaning in to enjoy Rudy's human scent, before his fingers dropped to grab the considerable flesh rising below. He knelt to examine the human cock in his hands: circumcised, impressive girth, the raw pinkness of healthy meat that deserved to be devoured raw. Van Cortlandt sniffed at the saline encrusted tip, amused by the seashore smell of seaweed rotting in the sun, so different from the clear, scentless ectoplasm his warlock brethren discharged. And they would surely be judging him, those who were lucid enough to notice he was servicing a human. But wiser warlocks understood; when one of their kind exchanged seed with a human, a bond was formed. The man sheds his ordinary, blind past, and can see enchantments otherwise invisible to mankind. Aging decreases, beauty is enhanced. A natural desire to serve and please the warlock becomes a defining purpose. Van Cortlandt's jaw slackened as he took Rudy to his root.

The wolves formed a tight, panting knot of fur. It was hard to tell where one animal ended and the other began. Marcus was delirious as another wolf mounted him roughly. This time there was no pain; he was completely lubricated by the remaining semen from an unknown number of previous partners. He howled as the wolf rocked away. Another licked

his face in brotherhood or sympathy. His red member ached for release. His paws rested on a napping wolf; the satiated beast yawned, oblivious to the surrounding orgy. An occasional goblin would get too close to the wolf-circle and howls of delight would turn to growls of menace. Through the smoke and candlelight, Marcus could see no exit, only the watchful forms of imposing warlocks. He was trapped. He shuddered as the wolf at his back shot his load and pushed off. Before Marcus could turn to search for a suitable mate another animal forcefully mounted him and bit down on his ear to guarantee compliance. Drool from the other wolf flowed down his muzzle like syrupy tears. His howl of grief was lost in a chorus of joy.

Rudy closed his eyes. The richness of the smoke was as intoxicating as the mouth of the man who had his head buried in his lap. No, not a man, a warlock. He was neither afraid nor concerned. He did not feel he had been drawn into the world of Faery Folk, but that his lack of paths, his listless life, left him no alternative. The warlock's blonde hair was fine and soft. Rudy stroked him, keeping rhythm as he felt his orgasm mounting. A magical tongue teased the proud vein that ran up the underside of his cock. The warlock pulled at his own long, thin wand. Dexterous fingers played with supple foreskin to reveal a soft, arrow-like head. Rudy's mouth was dry. He was thirsty for the warlock and hastened his own orgasm, so he could have the

208

chance to taste his new master. His testicles tightened as he flexed his thighs to signal an impending eruption. Van Cortlandt stretched his neck in accommodation. Rudy moaned and arched his back. Two senior warlocks watched approvingly and shot into the mouths of their ready goblins as Van Cortlandt swallowed Rudy's essence.

Rudy took the warlock's soft hand in his rough one and helped him up as he in turn lowered himself. The warlock's crotch was practically hairless. Rudy placed his cheek against his smooth flat stomach and inhaled the warlock's rich and alien musk. His slim erection wavered, expectant, beside the length of Rudy's nose. And Rudy moaned; his parted lips sought Van Cortlandt's cock. This was not a sexual act. He tasted the initial effervescence of pre-cum and knew this was a sacrament.

Marcus angrily broke free of yet another wolf humping at his backside. Desperate, he circled the other wolves and growled threateningly at them. His engorged cock was fraught with semen; long-thwarted lust goaded him on; a wolf unawares lapped at the furry sheath of wolf on its back. With animal accuracy, he lunged and planted his hungry cock firmly into the surprised wolf. Both yelped; Marcus in ecstatic relief, the other wolf in surprise and anger. Claws wild on stone, he struggled to find footing as the wolf resisted and tried to escape. Marcus

growled his intent. Submit! His teeth on the back of the other wolf's neck sank deeper in confirmation. The wolf whimpered, and Marcus began to rhythmically pump, his tongue hanging out.

With each gleeful thrust, Marcus unknowingly forgot something. Language slipped away as he rode the now compliant wolf. He forgot that he used to have a job and that he used to live indoors. He and his momentary paramour panted in unison. His teeth loosened their grip. As cum pulsed out of his animal cock, he forgot his name. He gave a long, poignant howl as the wolf beneath him broke free and scampered away. He searched the smoky atmosphere for the moon but found only darkness. His eyes reflected an internal wilderness so vast and dense that nothing human could ever find its way out.

Van Cortlandt dressed. His new valet held his cloak while he buttoned his shirt. Departing owls punctured the cloudy smoke, dissipating the charmed layer above. Goblins slinked back through the cracks. Their black semen spotted the boots of several warlocks now conversing over a flute of wine. Young warlocks feigned disinterest, but everyone knew that the evening had been a success. He told Rudy to open the cage door as he willed the wolves to enter. This time he had trouble differentiating the werewolf from the pack. The beast had

surrendered to the animal within and was thus now completely under his control. But this was no time to rest on his laurels. He quickly moved to blow out the black candles and thus conserve the extremely rare dragon elements. Exhausted and hungry, the wolves filed into the cage. Rudy stood naked and resolute, manning the cage door. They smiled slightly at each other. Much was still to be discussed between them, much more to be shared privately. Van Cortlandt snatched some empty vials from his work table and bent to gather the wolf semen cooling on the stone floor. Surely the younger warlocks will later privately deride him, he thought as he then moved to scrape a prodigious amount of goblin spunk from a warlock's boot, but it was not yet midnight, and a warlock's work is never done.

Having paid admission, rushing past the four suspicious eyes of Janus, Renaud and Barrett quickly made for the basement. Foraging a subterranean field of flesh, they pushed though a crop of clammy knees and elbows, sweat-slimmed limbs and hollow sighs. A roiling sea grudgingly parted to make way for their intrusion. A bewildered faun looked up. Barrett leaned in. It wasn't Christopher. A few naked men rose to contest the disturbance. Renaud stood still, clenching and unclenching his fists. Eyes closed, he called forth the change from within. As he began to shift, the men about the room took notice; some froze at the impossible sight. A werewolf in

Pluto's Basement? Others, terror-stricken, scrambled to find their waylaid clothes. While curious fauns gathered supplicants on dirty knees waited for what they imagined would be a treacherous treat. It was a first for Renaud while in wolf form. His concerns were not erotic. His sole drive was to interrupt this bacchanal and thwart a life-altering kiss. As his broadening back shredded his shirt, he let loose an angry howl, giving pause to the various orgies and entanglements. Barrett broke away to scour the smaller rooms and darker spaces. Would one become Christopher's cell? Had the deed already occurred? He pulled a coupling faun and human apart. The slick sound of the man's withdrawn erection bouncing off his stomach, his cry of dismay, coupled with the boy's gasp, all were drowned-out by the roar of the werewolf interloper amid rising murmurs and complaints (and Barrett wondered if, luck being on their side, Pluto might be too large to make it down the stairs).

With the added thought of possibly having to face a pissed-off god heavy on his mind, he turned to renew his search, peering closely at the faun groping toward his puzzled human partner. His lost, unfocused eyes shone in the gloom, clouded by the cataracts of an unquenchable desire. How long had he been down here, an hour, a decade, chained by longing to these grimy floors? Barrett pushed through to the next room, now wildly tearing at couples, desperately screaming Christopher's

name. Blinking fauns looked up. Angry, challenging men rose and sat back down at the sight of the towering werewolf, seething over the offending faun's shoulder.

In the corner of a dim grotto, Christopher moaned, chest heaving. He was lost in the sweaty administrations of several men holding his arms and legs apart. One huge, bullish, thick-browed man-beast hovered near Christopher's face, naked and half-aroused. The faun looked dazed. The man-bull's long, snaky cock draping over his shoulder, its foreskin tapered, frayed and dirty as an oil lamp's ever-moist and oft-lit wick; the beast leaned in for a cold kiss. The Dark Wolf roared. Fear rippled through the room. Dully, the man looked up. His blunted nose pierced, a dull gold ring hung heavy, a symbol of bovine servitude. Obtuse eyes narrowed below a low, bulbous brow. Thick, fleshy lips pulled back in silent protest across large yellow teeth. With this welcoming smile, it was apparent the creature did not see the werewolf as a threat, but as a challenge. Roughly, he shoved off from the faun and stood. Christopher bleated in pain as his head hit the cold cement floor.

Now Pluto might not have been able to navigate the narrow stairwell, but his servant Janus ably took to the steps.

The werewolf Renaud sensed this rocketing presence with just enough time to move out of the way; twisting his torso he shook out his claws, steadying himself to take aim. With a redoubled roar he thought to simultaneously lance each monster between his prospective ribs, but lupine instinct gave him pause. Janus chose to confront the rising Minotaur, now revealed in full, splendid height as the infamous rival bouncer from the notorious Meatpacking District sex club, The Labyrinth.

The two Behemoths stood close, sizing each other up. They locked in a powerful embrace. Janus fell to his knees, twin mouths, each mocking the other, dual grimaces of desire long withheld. The Minotaur ran his powerful, exploratory hands all over Janus' body, calloused fingers measuring the strength of his adversary. The two-faced bouncer kissed and licked the iron-like plates of the man-bull's taut abdominal muscles; his fat mammalian cock rose to prod at the hollow of Janus' cheek. Janus' own erection sprung strong and pink, like the ragged bud of a fiery orchid chewed to the stem by nocturnal teeth. Two vulnerable sighs (three really, counting the Janus' dual exhalations) filled the room. Theirs was an explosive joining, a deep, mutual elation; these giants patrolling their separate underworlds had never previously partnered with a creature of identical strength and girth. Their binary lust heated the basement; Renaud began to perspire as Barrett gathered

Christopher in his arms. He looked the boy in the eyes. He was scared, mouth open, moving but soundless, a small cave at sea-level, momentarily only able to echo the assault of the tide. His eyes, however, held no gloss, were not yet fogged by servility. Sure, his body was battered; his lips and buttocks were bruised, swelling from forced entry. But Christopher had yet to be kissed in the underworld.

Barrett cradled him in his arms and searched the room for the way out. All about forms and shapes continued to grasp at one another. Heads bobbed, limbs unfolded – the drama and violence before them an interlude only, nothing could call off such dark sport.

In their fast quest to find Christopher, they had become lost, disorientated. Barrett looked at Renaud with growing uncertainty, each wondering what other minions Pluto commanded in these sweaty depths. The treble of a distant spark caught their attention, erupting into the full flare of emancipation:

EXIT

The sign, previously dim, was all but unnoticeable when entering the basement. Long imprisoned, a lone, durable pixie took up their plight, providing the one thing desperately lacking

in the underworld. Light. They sped toward the newly illuminated staircase. And as he mounted the stairs, Renaud took aim and unhinged the antiquated sign with a well-placed swipe of his claw. The rusty prison fell. An unshackled pixie hovered, hesitant and bewildered. Then, with an appreciative burst of light, as groans and shielding arms went up throughout the chamber, the freshly unfettered pixie shot like a determined comet, weaving out of Pluto's Basement in a blaze of liberty. The boys and their werewolf ally were not far behind. Oblivious, the subterranean titans groped one another; the forms about them clambered to regain their collective grip on the shifting madness that carpeted the room. And the room settled. It was as if a passing motorboat had rudely disturbed the seabed; limbs again undulated like seaweed, rhythmically reaching for an intangible lust, mouths opened and closed like blind coral flowers, salting a black ocean with their sighs.

Outside, Renaud immediately shifted to human form. This was a terrible exertion without the naturally clandestine woodland conditions of the park. Still, the three of them were quite a sight: a tall, fatigued man in shredded clothes accompanied by a huffing faun struggling under the weight of a wane, unconscious youth cradled in his arms. A sight to stop traffic, as Renaud had hoped. He stepped out in front of a coasting taxi cab and raised his hand in a commanding gesture.

Hitting the breaks, the stunned satyr behind the wheel stared as Renaud motioned Barrett to ease Christopher into the backseat of the cab. Without taking his eyes off the driver, he joined them, his still-not-entirely human voice growling orders to head downtown.

Epilogue: Reel Around the Fountain

Wild boys always shine.

– Duran Duran

Morning. The unfamiliar joy of waking up beside someone kept Barrett from dozing off again. Renaud had stayed the night – their first date had been an extenuated adventure that had obviously exhausted them both. Barrett spent an hour examining the sleeping form beside him in the lazy, mote-filled light. Renaud's calm chest expanded and contracted peacefully with each breath, his ready nipples cresting like chocolate buoys atop twin caramel bays of confidence – the tight swirls of hair bunched within the muscular folds of his exposed underarms clutched a radiant darkness.

A perpetual breeze wafting through the bedroom window delivered a slight, permanent chill, heralding the coming change of seasons. Leaves would soon yellow and fall. As the foliage of the Ramble thinned, nature's curtain withdrew; it would be too cold for fauns to forage, and werewolves would grumble, uncomfortable without the camouflage of dense underbrush. And so the hunt was abandoned by all. As autumn turned to winter the natural tendency of fauns was to nestle down in groups and hibernate, a pile of snoring boys, a tangle of goat legs in a perpetual tug-of-war beneath weathered quilts. Only occasionally, might a faun be spotted outside, skipping across Eighth Avenue, kicking up a swirl of frost while traipsing to a bodega for a quart of milk, a quick snack before returning to a months-long slumber (though Barrett dreamily thought he might suffer a coat and kilt to make the cross-town bus and visit Renaud in his cozy little shop).

In winter, Werewolves fully retire their animal souls, tucking them deep into the folds of their spines while they continue to operate in the human world. On the coldest night of the year, when the moon is low and pregnant over the city, a lone wolfish man might take to the roof of his apartment building, lapels up, hands in his pockets, forlornly howling a mournful howl. Belatedly another soulful cry will go up,

delivered from another rooftop, too far off to bridge the cold solitude.

And so a segment of the city retires; the enchanted in respite until spring.

"Eventually, I'll have to rouse Renaud," he thought. He imagined them showering off their sleepy dross and heading out for breakfast. But not before he scoured the apartment for a marker and fresh paper, to make a quick sign: Room for Rent. Tradition among the rotating roster of fauns who have filled the apartment was to post vacancy notices at the Eighth Avenue bus stop.

Lying back in bed, Barrett stifled a yawn, imagining what manner of new faun would respond to the ad. Suddenly, he was excited at the prospect of a new roommate and leapt from his bed. Going to check on Christopher, he was surprised to discover the faun was not in his room.

Far above the street, hovering on the fire-escape outside his window, Christopher swayed with the wind. Then he sprung. A large woman clutched her grocery bag to her chest in surprise as the faun landed silently before her. Darting like a sparrow, Christopher was off -leaping down street, oblivious to the unlikely strand of epithets unspooling after him. He deftly

hop-scotched wilting parking meters, a blonde blur whizzing past delivery men; overtaxed dog walkers pulled at their charges as the excited canines chomped at the sudden wind.

Christopher was struck by a green fever. Something elemental claimed him, changed him. His cheeks narrowed while his eyes were wide, at full sail. His pupils were withdrawn; tiny red veins stretched across each white globe like childish hands reaching for the moon. He was a faun possessed, as if drawn back toward Park Life by some huge and invisible magnet buried somewhere in the Ramble. A Faery Compass called him and others.

Possibly this pole of enchantment sensed the coming autumn, the muting power of dead leaves and then snow; rather than surrender it struck its own bell early and long. This beckoning pulse reached the youngest fauns first, silent ripples pulled them from their slumber, easily prying them from dull jobs. All over the island-city men, too, received the call. Lured from their offices by the pocketful, divining rods thickened in their pants, fur erupted across their wrists, stray cufflinks shot across the room. Meetings prematurely adjourned, tugging at their ties they walked briskly toward the park. And it was only noon.

Racing through traffic, straddling the hoods of taxis, pirouetting off lamp posts with an astounding, newfound agility, Christopher shed emerald droplets. The sweat pouring off him smelled like freshly cut grass, every drop that hit the ground burrowed into the street by its heat alone. Tiny flowers, belligerent hard poppies, sprouted soon after. Rebounding beneath the crush of tires these flowers sprung fully formed, as white and ready as teeth on a baby shark.

Nightfall, the poppies explode like teardrops. Traffic pushes the serrated petals and leaves into the asphalt, pressing green arrows into the world, marking as permanent and right the paths to all desire.

About the Author

Tom Cardamone lives and writes in Brooklyn. He has published numerous short stories and book reviews. *The Werewolves of Central Park* is his first published novel. You can read more about him and his work at www.pumpkinteeth.net

ring any underwear. "Excuse me," I said, having a hard time loo
inded by that bulge in his crotch, "but don't I know you?" "Maybe
nd of to _____ bout
ith Ray _____ God,
loser? _____ in?" I
id. "Lik _____ stror
e body _____ e on C
ly, he I _____ I eve
up to t _____ any id
staking _____ e san
, I coul _____ ery lo
ood rac _____ e sw
ng with _____ e in s
ve go _____ behir
ill see _____ in pu
d?" he _____ vent t
rivacy, _____ grabl
hard. I
k, traci _____ t, so
ed it, ha
with my _____ bing
bing, I _____ n coc
e sound of unzipping filled the small space. I don't know who's I
but before I knew it, I had his rod in my hand, and mine was in hi
t to do?" he asked, his tone challenging. I knew exactly, and sank